"David is apprehensive about going off to the woods with his father. The dangers the two encounter, the change in the relationship between father and son are perceptively described. A fine book. Recommended."—*Bulletin of the Center for Children's Books*

"A heart-warming story about a boy from a broken home and the rugged, outdoorsman father he barely remembers. Suspense, mystery, and excitement." (Starred Review)— *Library Journal*

"The tightly-knit plot, including tense tangles with a grizzly, reveals that David can do things he thought he couldn't. An unusual story."—Chicago *Tribune*

"A story of two personalities exploring and learning to appreciate each other. Completely realistic."—*Horn Book*

"A suspenseful and believable story."—*ALA Booklist*

"Exciting, and very perceptive."—*Parents' Magazine*

"Very good psychology, fine outdoor detail, plus believable realism."—*America*

THE GRIZZLY

Also by the Same Authors

THE BLACK SYMBOL
TORRIE
THE BEARCAT
THE RESCUED HEART
PICKPOCKET RUN
WILDERNESS BRIDE
A GOLDEN TOUCH
THE BURNING GLASS

A HARPER TROPHY BOOK

HARPER & ROW, PUBLISHERS

THE GRIZZLY

by Annabel and Edgar Johnson

Pictures by Gilbert Riswold

THE GRIZZLY

Copyright © 1964 by Annabell J. and Edgar R. Johnson

Library of Congress Catalog Card Number: 64-11831

ISBN 0-06-440036-0

First printed in 1964. 7th printing, 1971. Large type edition printed in 1966.

For Ursula

CONTENTS

Part One : FEAR

Chapter 1

Fear . . . sometimes it is a swift thing. But there are times when it is more like a great dark clock, ticking. To David it came that way, out of long-ago years he could hardly remember. For months it would be quiet inside him as his own heartbeat. Then he would have one of the nightmares.

He would dream that he was in some lonely place, listening for danger—a man's footsteps pacing toward him. The tall figure would loom up in the darkness, just a silhouette with no real face but bristling pale brows and a glint of teeth in a crooked smile. Slowly he would come closer—and David would wake up trembling.

Even after he was awake he would lie there pulsing with fear, remembering that the shadowy figure had been real once. Because the man in his dreams was his father.

The word seemed strange when David spoke it silently to himself: Father. Other people had dads, nice men who took them places on Sunday, to a ball game or a movie. When other kids bragged, "My pop and me are going to build a boat this summer," David had sort of envied them, but it was a far-off feeling.

Whenever he thought about his own father, the dark image rose in his mind, making him shiver, even in broad daylight. He wasn't sure why—he couldn't remember too clearly all the bad things that had happened in those early days before his father had gone away. He only knew he dreaded the time when the nightmare man would come back and he would have to meet him face to face.

Now the day had come—so soon. Much sooner than he'd reckoned. There had been the letter first, and then the phone call. Mother looking nervous. Finally she had told him, "Your father is in town. He wants to see you—he wants to take you camping this weekend."

David had tried to brace himself. But he felt pretty puny—all loose and scared inside. He had wished for more time, wished he could grow some more before he had to meet this moment. If he just were taller and didn't perspire so much—right now his hands were wet, clenched in his pockets. And under the new blue-checked shirt he could feel the prickle of sweat.

Because this was no dream, now. Right this minute he and this stranger who was his father were sitting here only an arm's reach apart. Just the two of them, busting along in this pickup truck at sixty miles an hour, away from home and the city. Going up into the high mountains together.

Cautiously David risked a sidelong glance at the man behind the wheel. With a grim sort of wonder he marveled at how clearly it was coming back to him—the look of the lean face with its jutting blond brows, frowning against the glare of the afternoon sun. He remembered that frown, all right, but it wasn't half as dangerous as the crooked smile.

He even remembered the powerful-looking hands that gripped the wheel. The arms that showed beneath the rolled-up shirtsleeves were tough as leather. Every movement was so sure—the way the man stuck two fingers into his shirt pocket and got out a pack of cigarettes, shook one loose. The way he struck a light from a kitchen match with his thumbnail. Dropping his hand to the wheel again, he spun

5

it easily to swerve the truck off the highway onto a side road.

It was one of those gravel roads, worn down to the ribs. The pickup jarred along it like a jackhammer. In the haze of dust David glimpsed a sign—ENJOY YOUR NATIONAL FOREST—then it was gone.

When they topped a rise in the land he glanced back uneasily. Couldn't even make out where the highway was now. Dense pine woods had folded in around them, stretching off on all sides, rising to timberline on the high peaks to the west. Barren and raw, the range was still wearing heavy patches of snow. From back in the city the mountains looked flat, as if they were painted on the sky. Now they took on a terrible, beautiful sharpness—white rimrock towering above ragged deep canyons. A wilderness except for a few rough-cut roads like this one.

They hadn't passed a car since they left the highway. Not many people came up here this early in the season. David shuddered slightly. The man beside him glanced over. Deep under the brows his eyes were a burning blue, like the heart of the match when it had flared.

"You cold or something?" he asked.

"No, sir." David sat stock-still. He hadn't supposed his father was even thinking about him. It was as if they had been traveling through a huge

6

emptiness—together, but a long way apart. Now, suddenly the truck seemed small and close, stifling with silence.

More memory was beginning to come back, of days when he was little. Fierce words and rough hands. Practically the earliest recollection David had was of being hit. His father jabbing him, poking him in the chest like a boxer. With that grin, saying, "Come on, boy, hit back! Hit back hard!" Once a blow had caught David on the nose—blood all down his shirt front. He could still hear his mother crying, "Stop it, Mark. Stop!"

And there'd been a steel bar in the back yard—he suddenly remembered that. How high it had seemed when his father had lifted him up there, saying in that tough way of his, "Go on, boy, you've got to learn to hang on." And when he had fallen off and gotten the wind knocked out of him, how he had choked to get his breath back. His mother had screamed then, too. "He's too young, Mark!"

There had been a lot of bad times in those days, dangerous times. Something had happened near some deep water—David couldn't quite remember what it was, but just thinking about it made his heart pound. He could still see the black ripples, sipping, sipping. . . .

He tried to shove the old memories away. Maybe

the dreams had been wrong. He tried to tell himself this was just an ordinary guy, driving along, coat off, hat tipped back on his head, necktie loose and askew. *What's to be scared of?*

Besides, I'm older now. I'm going on twelve, David told himself firmly, and that's fairly old. Old enough to have your own allowance and a good pocket knife, and go downtown by yourself. And not take anything off other guys around school. Old enough not to be afraid of people—

And then he caught a faint reflection of himself in the window glass—lank dark hair and eyes sprung wide with foreboding. A broad mouth pressed too tight. He licked his lips and tried to sit easier. *If there's one thing you don't want to do, it's to let anybody know you're worried.* It's like being nervous about dogs; if they sense it they get meaner.

He looked beyond his own image, out at the dense woods all around them. They went past another dirt road—To Trapper's Creek the sign said. The name jolted him all over again. There had been a fuss about that at home this morning before they left. . . .

David saw it again—the three of them standing around the living room, being polite. When his father had arrived, Mother had even smiled in a funny sort of way—David thought she was scared, too. He himself had felt awkward in his new clothes, with the cuffs of the blue jeans stiff as cardboard around his ankles. Mother had looked crisp, too, in a new dress. He wondered why she had gotten so fixed up, since she wasn't going with them. But there they had stood, she and David, side by side, facing the tall man. And David could sense how fluttery she was.

Trying to sound calm, she had asked, "Where will you take David? I'd like to know, Mark."

And his father had answered in an even tone, low as the hum of a big engine. "Who knows where the fishing will look best? Maybe Trapper's Creek—"

"Not Trapper's!" she had burst out quickly. Then trying to sound reasonable, she went on, "It's just that some men got snowed in up there this time last year."

"Snow—" Mark shrugged.

That had upset her even more. "David's just a little boy. I won't have you putting him through some ordeal!"

Remembering, David flushed with embarrassment all over again. A wonderful mother—the kindest, best—but of all times to call him a "little boy."

It had galled his father, too. He had said roughly, "Maybe you expect us to go fishing in the back yard? Jeanne, I can't draw you a map of my plans. The court has granted me this weekend with my son and

I'm taking him. That is, if he's willing. Well, David?"
He spoke the name with a quick uppercut on the last
syllable—it was like a dare.

So here they were, and they had just gone past the
turn-off to Trapper's Creek, and Mark's jaw was
knotted tight and hard. David could even guess what
he was thinking.

From years ago a terrible sentence came to hang
in the air—the last thing his father had said before he
went away for good:

"I warn you, Jeanne, you'll turn this boy into a
sissy!"

Worse than some sort of threat, it was like an awful
prediction. And David knew—as he stared out at
the wild country he *knew*—that his father hadn't forgotten that.

Chapter 2

If you want to go to Trapper's Creek, I don't give a darn about a little snow. David wished he had said it, just like that, manly and cool. He never could seem to think of the right thing in time. But if it wasn't going to be Trapper's, then where?

Apparently his father had something in mind. He had slowed the truck, now. Right in the middle of nowhere he was scanning the edge of the road. At a certain spot he turned off and drove straight into the forest.

They were on a faint old track—nobody had used it in years. Snaking between the tall pines it was choked with dry brush that tore at the underside of the truck. On either hand, branches clawed the windows. Looked as if it might dead-end any minute.

But Mark drove right on as if he knew where he was going.

David watched him with secret misgivings. There was a look of satisfaction in that stern face. He must have been intending to come here all along. But why wouldn't he just say so, then?

Mark glanced over at him swiftly, and David let go of the door handle. Hadn't realized he was hanging on to it so hard. His father's expression took on a shade of amusement.

"Good thing to get away from crowds," he remarked. "Fishing's better back in here, too."

"Yes, sir." David was remembering—his mother had told him to be polite, and he would. But he had a feeling he'd better answer up firmly.

"Ever been fishing?" Mark asked carelessly.

David thought back quickly to last summer, when he and some of the other guys had messed around in the irrigation canal. Never did catch anything. "Yes, sir," he said, "I've done a little."

Mark seemed surprised. "Fly fishing?"

"I use worms." David didn't mean it to sound smart, but it came out too loud.

"You'll like flies better," Mark told him flatly. "More sport to it. Idea is to outsmart the fish. Take a hook with some feathers tied to it, make him think it's a real insect."

12

David had looked at trout flies in the sporting goods store. Never could see much to them. Now a worm must smell good, probably even tasted good to a fish.

"Of course fly-casting is harder." Mark shot him another keen look. Like a jab in the ribs. *I dare you!*

It brought back to David his mother's warning. This morning before his father had come she had looked at David in that fond, troubled way.

"You mustn't be afraid of him," she'd said. "He won't hurt you. In fact he's not really harsh—in most ways he's a fine person. And I don't think he's ever been afraid of anything in his life. He's so strong—" Her eyes had quickened with an excitement that David had never seen before. Then she looked away. "So strong himself that he never has understood any sort of weakness."

"I'm not so weak," David had protested. "I can do ten pushups."

"He'd expect you to do twenty—or maybe fifty. That's what I'm trying to say," she explained hurriedly. "If he tries to goad you into doing something beyond your strength, you must simply say no. Politely—no. Your father has curious ways of testing people."

And David was beginning to have a strong hunch that Mark had something on his mind, all right—something bigger than fishing. To go to all this effort,

driving miles and miles into the deep part of the forest. What had he said? "...can't draw you a map of my plans." All at once the words took on an ominous ring. David thought this must be what was bothering his mother, too. Not some off-chance of a late spring snowstorm, but a nameless, lurking suspicion of trouble.

Mark was going on now about fishing. "...Pretty early in the season for insects. May be some hatches, though." He broke the sentences off in short chunks as if he weren't used to talking much—not to kids, anyway. "In fly fishing you go in pursuit of the trout. You don't just sit on the bank, dunking worms. You walk, casting as you go. You wade the stream, if necessary, to reach the fish's hideout, tempt him out

of it. Get him to strike. In a sense, you stalk him."

There was a zest in the way he spoke that made David want to wriggle. Wild animals stalk things. When he saw a tree fallen across the track ahead, in a rush of relief he blurted out, "The road's blocked! I reckon we'll have to go back."

His father braked the car and eyed him briefly. "You let every little thing keep you from going where you want, you'll never get anywhere." Reaching under the seat, he found an ax and got out. For a minute he stood there sizing up the problem, unbuttoning his shirt with impatient little thrusts of his fingers. Then stripping it off, he hefted the ax.

With uneasy fascination David watched. Those shoulders looked as solid as if they'd been chipped out of rock, except that the muscles slid and rippled as Mark lit into the fallen pine. His blade rose and fell in a long, deadly sweep—chips sprayed right and left. Distantly David thought of all the men he had seen in gym suits at the dads-and-teachers volleyball tourney up at school last fall. Skinny arms and bulging stomachs, and they were so pale under their clothes. Mark's torso was an even, deep bronze. The kind that comes from years of working under the sun.

My father? He's in Africa right now, doing some engineering. David had told people that a hundred times. It always made a good excuse because it was

16

the truth, and he didn't have to go on and mention that his parents were separated.

He hadn't really pictured how hot it must be over there in the desert, though. Mark's brush-cut hair was a scorched straw color. Without his hat and shirt he was a fierce-looking man. David could imagine what a stir he would have caused, mixing with the others at the volleyball game. Kids would have stared. "Who's he?" And David would have said casually, "Yeah, that's my dad. . . ."

With a crack and a crash the tree trunk fell in two. Mark laid hold of the upper part and heaved it aside far enough for the truck to pass. Without bothering to put on his shirt again, he came back and swung in behind the wheel. After all that, he wasn't even breathing very hard—not sweating a bit. Beside him, David felt narrow and moist.

As they drove on he was thinking back numbly to the volleyball tourney—and all the other times when he'd been the only one without a father. Times when some kid would say, "I'm going fishing this weekend with my pop." And David had pictured himself just loafing off with some nice good-natured fellow. It could have been fun.

And fathers could tell you about a lot of things if they were the right kind. David had often thought that if he'd had somebody to practice with, he might have made the baseball team. Instead—well, he always did freeze up at tryouts. He had missed an easy fly ball and when he'd come up to bat, he had struck out. Looked clumsier than he really was. He shot a regretful glance at Mark. *I wanted to make that team, too!*

His father was driving faster now, guiding the truck expertly over the uneven track. All around them the woods were dusky, though the sky was still full of light. And then, as if they had suddenly come through the end of a long tunnel, they burst forth into the open. Flanked by mountains on either side, they were in a valley. For miles it spread out around them, in winter-brown grassland. Curving through it, a young river lay like a sheet of dark glass.

Twilight had fallen here below, but a soft brilliance still lay over the land, an afterglow from the golden furrows of cloud above. On the far side of the valley a great cliff rose, a sheer rock face towering a thousand feet, afire with sunset.

Mark guided the truck off across the broad meadow and cut the engine. In the stillness, small earth noises rose around them—the faint clash of dry grasses rubbing shoulders in the drift of the evening wind. From a hundred feet away came the mutter of the stream.

"Nobody here." Mark seemed to speak it almost

18

to himself. Staring up at the cliff, his high-boned face was ruddy from its light. "Nobody but us."

"Who lives down that way?" David made a random motion toward the far end of the valley. But you could see it was deserted.

Mark fixed him with the kind of thoughtful look he had given the tree. David was pinned and held.

What does he want? What do they ever want— grown-ups with their questions, their tests? They never explain what they're getting at, they just watch you like that!

"You don't mind, do you? Being here by ourselves?" Mark's tone was too quiet to tell whether he was taunting.

"I like to be alone!" David claimed defiantly, his voice bursting high and shrill upon the stillness.

"Maybe . . . you'd rather be here *all* alone?" Mark was beginning to grin—a strange one-sided smile. The nightmare smile, but somehow worse. Because there wasn't going to be any waking up out of this one.

Chapter 3

"Now then, David. Choose a couple of flies—whatever looks best to you."

"They're all very—nice." David stared down at the open tackle box. He was thinking fast. It was beginning to take shape in his mind, what this secret plan of his father's might be. "It might take me a while to learn to use them, though. So maybe—it's so late—maybe you'd rather do some fishing yourself right now."

Mark seemed impatient. "Yes, of course it's late. But I can give you a quick run-down on how to handle your rod."

"I don't always—seem to get the hang of things like fishing."

"There's nothing 'like' fishing!"

"I mean sports. I got a D in phys. ed. at school last semester."

"If you're not good, the idea is to get good."

"Yes, sir. Only I—I could watch you for a while first."

When Mark finally strode off toward the river alone, David loosened up and slumped a little inside. It had been a tight few minutes. He wished he hadn't had to sound so dumb. Of all things on earth he hadn't meant to tell Mark, it was about that D. But there had been no time to consider his words. He had to make sure he didn't get drawn into going too far from the truck.

Because that was part of a scheme—he was almost sure. All the time Mark had been changing into his old clothes and setting up the rods, David had been thinking. About the way his father had looked when he said "*all* alone"—a teasing, challenging look, sort of sizing him up. *Curious ways of testing people. . . .* And what would be a slicker way for Mark to test a person's gumption than to lure him downstream a way, then sneak back and just drive off and leave him?

All alone . . . for how long? Overnight? Or maybe until Sunday. See if David could catch his own food, see how he'd take care of himself? Or if he'd panic? The cold steel of the truck body was biting through the thin shirt—David was leaning back against it

21

hard. Going to stick to this old pickup like a coat of paint. *But I can't! He's looking back right now. I'm supposed to be following. Watching.*

Mark had waded into the water, current boiling around the rubber hip boots he wore—he glanced over his shoulder again. David busied himself, putting on his heavy wool jacket. But that only took so long. At last there was nothing else to do but play this fearsome game. He left the truck and drifted warily across the meadow toward the river.

Pausing on the bank, he viewed the tumbling water uneasily. That channel was faster than he'd thought, sweeping hard between rocks, swirling backward into deep pools. In one place it was almost overflowing the bank, fingering to find any little soft spot where it could break through. David wondered why the sick sense of dread came over him. It was strange—he wasn't afraid of just any water. He had learned to swim in the YMCA pool, like everybody else. All the same he knew that nothing on earth was going to make him wade into that river.

In the stillness his own pulse thumped hard in his ears. It was quieter here than any place he'd ever been. The birds had hushed; the fields seemed hardly to breathe. As evening settled in, the air was as clear as fresh-washed glass. It made everything vivid—the cliff, the meadow ringed around with woods. At some other time David would have even liked it here—a place so clean. But right this minute he would have welcomed an old tin can lying around. Or the sound of a plane flying over—anything that might mean other people weren't too far away.

He had reached a place where the river really was brimming out of its bank. It had turned a whole big patch of meadow soggy. David's sneakers were sinking in it—he retreated to dry ground in a hurry. Of course Mark had gone right on through—*tromp, tromp*—leaving deep bootholes. *Am I supposed to slog right on into the mud up to my knees?* Angry confusion welled up in him.

As he started to skirt the marsh David kicked at a clod of earth. Then stopped short. Because how did a clod get turned over out here? A whole patch of ground was dug up evenly as if somebody had been looking for worms. Some other fisherman? It must be!

So Mark was wrong. They weren't so alone after all. The knowledge steadied David; he could even take a deep breath again. Nice to discover that his father could be mistaken about something. Hopefully he scanned the darkening valley, half expecting to see a light somewhere below.

But the dusk was unbroken. Getting so thick it

23

was hard to see. As he hesitated, listening, he heard something moving over along the river bank. Peering hard, he could just make out the dim silhouette of his father coming back —a tall figure, moving through the shadows.

Chapter 4

First you scoop out a shallow hole about the size of a dishpan, arrange rocks around it—David tried to memorize each move his father was making. Then in the bottom of the hole put dry grass, and little sticks on that. Next some larger ones, and have a stack of the next size ready. Get out your match—except, suppose you haven't got one!

As Mark tossed the matchbox aside, David picked it up, fiddled with it carelessly, and managed to slip out about six without being noticed. He stuck them in his coat pocket and turned to watch. Because if there was a plan, it wasn't turning out the way he had figured it at first. Now he couldn't tell how it was going to be sprung on him, and that made him jumpier than ever. All he knew was that he'd darn well better learn to build a fire.

The grass crackled. Thin flames licked through the small sticks, snatching at the ones on top. With a *huff* the whole pile caught and blazed, casting a brightness up into Mark's somber face.

"You could get out the groceries." He glanced across at David. Seemed to be in a pretty good humor in spite of not having caught any fish yet. David was more sure than ever that there was some other real purpose to this trip. But what the next step would be—

With a kind of desperate reasoning he was trying to figure it as he went around to the back of the pickup. The truck bed was roofed over by an aluminum "camper"—a metal shell fastened onto the body. Inside was a tumble of junk—old clothes, bedrolls, frying pans and nets. David's overnight bag was there, a canvas kit that his mother had packed. He hoped she had put in his heavy flannel pajamas; the night air was growing cold.

As he got out the bag of groceries he was thinking of her sitting there at home, having dinner all alone. For a minute his whole longing stretched off across the miles. But he couldn't help her tonight, and she couldn't help him. Feeling older and wearier, he

26

went back to the fire and set down the food. Not that he was going to eat much of it. No appetite at all.

And yet when they got some strips of bacon frizzling on sticks over the fire, he began to feel a pang in his belly. The sight of the two open cans of beans bubbling, charring in the flames, was bound to make anybody's mouth water. He almost resented the rise of hunger.

"Hold your bacon over the can so the drippings get on the beans. That's the trick." Mark sounded friendly. So friendly it disturbed David. Ought to be on guard, he knew. But with the fire at his feet and food warming his belly, he felt almost comfortable.

"This is exactly what I had to eat," Mark went on, "when I made my first camp in this valley. Wasn't much older than you. I came in on foot—just roaming the mountains and here it was. Did you ever discover a place? Nothing can make you feel so much as if it's your own as having it all to yourself."

David came alert with a jolt. There it was again— the plan, showing around the edges of this brotherly talk. Anxiously he dug into the beans. If he was going to be left here to enjoy the valley all by himself it would be useful to have eaten a good supper. Several more strips of bacon, he decided.

Mark was watching with that uneven smile. "This

is happening just as I pictured it. Over there in the African desert, where it's so hot that you sweat and swelter, I knew that as soon as my contract was up, I was coming back here. To this spot. Just like this, on a cool night in late May. I knew I was going to bring you along too."

It gave David an odd feeling to learn that his father had been working on this clear over in Africa. Thinking that much about him . . .

"Why?" he asked frankly.

The question seemed to catch Mark off guard. "Well, when a man has a son—" he began. Then he said, "Put it this way: Didn't you ever wonder about me, all these years?"

"Yes, sir." David nodded. In the middle of the night. Lying there shaking with some fear he couldn't quite understand. The silence echoing with a clash of words he couldn't make out. He had wondered, all right, just what really had happened all those times when he was little.

"Did your mother ever talk about me?" Mark asked quietly.

David pretended for a minute to be eating. He wasn't going to give away anything about Mother. What he and she talked about was their own business. The truth was, she didn't speak much about Mark. Whenever she did, it brought a sadness over her that didn't leave for days. But his father was waiting for an answer.

"She said you gave us the money to live on," David admitted cautiously. Once she had even wondered if Mark was keeping enough for himself, he sent them so much. "She told me you were a good engineer."

His father seemed puzzled. "Didn't she tell you why I—I've been gone so long?"

"She never says anything bad about other people." It came out sounding pretty bald, but it was the truth.

Mark's face darkened. "There wasn't anything so very bad to tell. We just—differed. I thought it would be best for—everybody—if I took the job in Africa." Then his tone changed. "I'm sure she's been a fine mother to you. She's a wonderful, warm— But now you're of an age when you need to go places with a man once in a while. Learn to tackle something bigger than everyday problems. You ought to know how to get your own food. Make your way through a forest—"

David squirmed and got up. He went to throw his empty bean can in the trash box and Mark followed. Together they walked around to the rear of the pickup to get their bedding.

"I reckon I'll sleep inside." David peered into the truck.

"Nonsense! Half the pleasure is to lie under the

stars." Mark spoke sharply. David stiffened.

"Yes, sir." Which meant he was going to have to keep one eye open all night. Weary as he was, it wouldn't be easy. Thinking of that comfortable bunk-bed of his at home, he unfolded his pajamas . . . something fell out and rolled on the ground. Mark bent to scoop it up—a tin of ham.

"Did you put this in?" His brows drew together angrily.

David was too startled to do anything but tell the truth. "No, sir."

"Then your mother must have. I guess she thought— What the devil did she think?"

She must have been planning, too. As it dawned on David he felt a surge of gratitude, a proudness that almost choked him. He saw a vision of his mother, beautiful and anxious, with that can of ham in her hand, just slipping it in there with his clothes in case he might need it. Unsteadily he said, "There's a candy bar, too." It was right there under his extra socks.

Mark stood staring at the can absently. Then with a shrug he tossed it back into the open bag and hunkered down to spread out their bedrolls. David chewed his lip resentfully. Not that Mark had said anything against her; it was his look—sort of disgusted. David wanted to lash out and defend her, but he couldn't think how.

Still seething, he bundled himself into the sleeping bag. Lay there, rigid, shoulder bones and hips rebellious against the rough earth. The fire had burned out, glowing only once in a while when the wind fanned the coals.

As if some embers of his earlier thoughts still flickered, too, Mark spoke moodily out of the darkness. "To be really honest with this place we shouldn't even have brought beans. The old settler—the first man in here—he probably didn't have any such luxuries. His cabin's over there in the woods. It was his wagon track we followed in—part of it. He had to break trail sixty miles or more from the nearest trading post. Under those conditions you travel light and live by your wits. Catch fish, track down game, or starve." Then he added, "Mostly the old-timer thrived on solitude and silence. That's not for weak men; they need neighbors and noise."

David knew when he was being given a lesson. He couldn't resist the temptation to deflate it. "We've got a neighbor," he retorted. "And I'll bet he's a nice guy, too. He fishes with worms. So anyhow there is another way in here after all!" When the first word fell, the rest came crashing down like a stack of bricks. The whole secret was out.

Mark threw back his blankets and sat up. "What guy? You saw somebody around here?"

"I saw the place where he was digging for worms. You didn't. You went through the mud."

Mark got all the way up now and threw some sticks onto the coals. "Tell me from the beginning— what did you find? A hole of some sort? How deep?"

David grew interested. This was really bugging old Mark. "It was a big patch, all-over digging like a garden spaded up."

"You saw spade marks? Sharp cuts?"

That didn't sound just right. "More like with a fork—a pitchfork, I guess."

The fire had caught on. Its ruddy light streamed off Mark's lean flanks. He didn't wear pajamas, just his shorts, though the night was turning colder. Stars were scattered all over the sky like chips of ice. For a long moment he looked off down the valley. Then he stooped and began to pick up his bedding.

"Where are we going?" David got up, too. "Somewhere else?"

"I've decided we'll sleep in the truck tonight, after all."

"So there is another way in?" David tried not to sound too triumphant.

"No. No, there isn't." Mark seemed worried. Anyone else, you might even think he was upset. "Below here and to the east and west of us, the real

33

wilderness sets in—the wildest stretch of country in the state of Montana."

"And no neighbor or anything?"

Mark lifted the other sleeping bag and chucked it into the pickup. "I didn't say that."

Chapter 5

It was a different kind of dream. The tick of the clock was soft as the pad, pad of bare feet—not coming straight on—circling. David lay in the grip of the same old terror, but even in his dream he was somehow conscious of Mark asleep beside him. So this must be someone else who stalked through the grass. . . .

He struggled to wake up and escape it. Slowly the hard bed of the truck came into reality beneath him, the sleeping bag, the unfamiliar pillow. But still it seemed he heard the whisperous footfall. Opening his eyes, he started wide awake. A white brilliance was streaming in his face like a spotlight. The moon, a lopsided three-quarter moon, was shining in the window brighter than he'd ever seen it in his life.

Still dazed, he sat up, peering out the window. Half expected to see somebody out there moving across the meadow. But it lay deserted under the moonlight. After a while he sank down again, shivering, into his blankets. Not that he was going to get back to sleep. . . .

The next thing he knew, Mark was nudging him. "Wake up, David. Daylight's coming on. Best time for fishing."

Groggily he crawled out of his cocoon of bedding. The Levis were clammy, nasty things to put on bare legs. He found his shirt in the semi-dark, but one sneaker was missing. Finally located it under his bedroll—been sleeping on the fool shoe all night. Grumpy and sore, he followed Mark out into the gray dawn.

A mist lay over the valley. Wisps of it were rising off the river like slow steam. The hard cold of midnight had changed to a softer, wetter kind of chill. Fire didn't take hold very well, smoking and sputtering.

"Should I go look for some dry wood?" David fidgeted, about to start for the forest.

"No." Mark stopped him sharply. "We have enough. Anyhow it wouldn't be any drier." He was restless this morning, as if he thought something might happen. Sitting on his heels by the fire he made coffee quickly, spilling the stuff into the water, spoonful on spoonful.

"About today—" he began, then cocked a critical look at David. "You say you're not very good at athletics?"

"I usually get a C," David said, determined to set the record straight. "And I made a B in manual training. I like doing things with tools."

Mark made a short gesture as if he thought that was O.K. "But right now I'm more interested in your physical condition."

"I can do ten pushups." Not going to apologize for it, either.

"How fast can you run? What's your time for the hundred-yard dash?"

"Fourteen seconds." Never had gotten the knack of starting fast. The teacher was going to work with him on it, but there never was time.

"Ever play baseball? How's your arm? Can you peg a straight throw while you're on the run?"

"I'm only a substitute," David admitted gloomily. "I don't get much practice at fielding."

Mark snapped a stick in two and threw the pieces on the fire. "How good are you at climbing trees?"

And another chunk of memory fell in place like a piece in a jigsaw puzzle. Back when he was little there had been a pine tree somewhere. All at once

37

David could remember how the rough bark on the branches had scratched his hands as he tried to clamber up it. Slipped and skinned a knee. And then his mother had picked him up, holding him tightly. "He's too young, Mark! He could kill himself!" It all came back like a flash in the second he hesitated over his father's question.

Mark was getting impatient. "Put it this way: Do you think you *could* climb a tree if you wanted to?"

The truth was, David didn't see any around that he thought he could manage. Carefully he said, "I'd better not, sir. Mother doesn't like it."

Abruptly his father took the pot off the fire and poured boiling coffee into their cups. "Just above here, there's a big swampy area. I've seen moose there many a time. A cow moose protecting her calf can run the hundred in somewhat less than fourteen seconds. If one was charging, you might wish you could throw a rock straight enough to hit it and try to distract it. And if you couldn't make it up a tree, that might be the last race you ever engaged in."

The coffee was spreading warmth in the pit of David's belly. Pretty strong warmth. He wondered why Mother had never allowed him to drink it. This was the kind of thing you need on a cold wet morning. Especially if somebody is goading you.

With a touch of bravado he remarked, "I reckon

there's a lot of wild animals around here. Bears and mountain lions and—"

"You've got the idea." Mark nodded dryly. "The world is full of dangers. This afternoon we'll take this up again." He stood up and pitched the dregs of his coffee.

As David watched his father get out the rods and fly box he was thinking that if he had to shinny up and down the pines, this was going to turn into a rough day. Now Mark was unlocking another box, a heavy wooden one that was fixed in one corner of the pickup. Opening it, he took out a revolver in a holster and began to work his belt through the loops. For some reason David was reminded of stories of old-time gunmen, vigilantes who took the law into their own hands.

His uneasiness swelled as Mark drew the weapon from its leather case. David was hypnotized by the ugly beauty of the thing. He had never seen a gun this close before—cold blue metal and a wicked-looking grip. That round hole in the muzzle looked big as a cannon.

"Is that a police pistol?" he asked nervously.

"Much more powerful. It's a .357 Magnum." From a box Mark shook some bullets into his palm. Gleaming like little missiles, they had a deadly fascination too.

David stared as Mark fed them into the cylinder of the gun. "What do you need it for?"

"Just say I feel better with it on."

Better? Walking around, carrying such a dangerous thing? He hadn't worn it yesterday, before they'd talked about the neighbor. Last evening David had been glad to have another presence in the valley, but somehow his dream had changed that. It seemed ominous now, and it was clear that his father was troubled too, though he was trying not to let on.

Carelessly Mark asked, "By the way, where did you say that digging was?"

"Down there where the ground gets real wet. Only back, away from the river. Halfway over to the trees."

"Wait for me here. I think I'll take a look." With the gun slapping his thigh, Mark walked off into the mist.

Chapter 6

The fire made a small pinch of warmth in the vastness of the fog. David stood close by it, stamping his feet to get the blood back into them. His shoes were soaked from the wet grass—every blade strung with droplets. Around him out there in the haze the valley seemed to crouch, waiting. Even the mutter of the river was hushed in the ghostly white of dawn. David felt threatened.

Some new anxiety seemed to hover over him—something to do with that gun. He had an odd hunch that his father must know, or guess, who this neighbor was. Some old hunter, maybe, that he'd had trouble with before? Or a prospector who didn't want anybody horning in on his diggings?

Might be some gold around here. There were still

rich veins to be dug in these mountains, David knew. His mother had even gotten a book from the library on how to hunt for it. The thought of her came upon him suddenly, like a fever breaking through his inner chill. A feeling all mixed up with warm dry clothes and the hum of the furnace in the basement on a cold morning like this. She'd be sorry he'd slept so poorly. Wouldn't like that gun, either. Of course she was a girl; they aren't supposed to like a rough kind of life like this.

David squared his shoulders and shoved his hands in his pockets, staring out into the mist. In a minute he heard the heavy squish of rubber boots and made out the tall figure of his father striding across the meadow.

As he came up Mark said briskly, "Just about what I expected. This neighbor of ours is the four-footed kind. That digging was the work of a bear. Looks as if it was done a week ago or more. Nothing to get jittery over—he's probably miles away by now. What's the matter, don't you believe me?"

"Yes, sir. Only what would a bear be digging up?"

"Oh—field mice, gophers. Grubs, maybe. This time of year, right after hibernation, sometimes they eat roots. They're usually in a bad mood, too. So seeing that he might just still be around, and you don't climb trees or run very fast, I think you'd better do your fishing close by. Stick near the truck so you can get inside in a hurry if you see a wild animal coming."

Which was fine with David! It would put off the moment when they'd have a fuss about wading into that water. Soberly he nodded. "Whatever you say."

Not that he was taken in by this "bear" story. If there was nothing to worry over, why did Mark still wear the gun? And telling him to stay here—this was a lot different from yesterday. So the plot about sneaking away and deserting him—if there'd been one—must have been called off. In fact Mark's whole manner was different this morning, edgy and watchful.

"I don't recommend that you use flies," he was saying. "I'm going to, but there probably aren't any insects out yet on a day like this. Until the sun burns the mist off, you'd best stick with spinners or bait."

Trying to shame him, maybe? David wondered. Hinting that flies were too tough for him? It stung a little, but he tried not to show it.

"Reckon I'll dig some worms," he remarked.

"Certainly, if you like. But I'd advise you to try devil-scratchers first. They're the trout's natural food." As he put a fly on his line Mark kept glancing around, off upstream, then across the river. "After a week of full moonlight these fish have fed day and night until they're stuffed. That's probably why I didn't get a strike last evening. Now then, here's your rod."

In a few words he explained how the automatic reel worked. "Later on today I'll show you the knack of casting. For right now, just try to get your bait as far as you can from shore. Remember to keep a tight line on your fish. Don't hurry him. And once you've landed one, hit it on the back of the head with a stick, or against a rock. Kill it fast—don't let it choke to death on air. That's not sporting."

As he watched his father disappear into the fog, heading off downstream, David was repeating those last words to himself. "Kill it . . . hit it on the head . . . " He'd never really thought about what he would do once he did catch something. Not that he was especially fond of fishes, but just to kill a thing . . . ?

Suddenly he wasn't in too much of a hurry to start. He stared down at the tackle box open on the tailgate of the truck. Ought to put one of those darn flies on, just to show Mark. All this fuss he was making—and over what? David picked out one of the flies. Who ever heard of a real insect with a pink silk body and a collar of brown fuzz? He put it back; better not mess with it.

There were only two spinners in the box—big, fancy,

bright pieces of brass with red beads and neat little swivels on the end. *It would be my luck*, he thought, *to toss one out there and tangle it up on a rock, the first cast.* He laid the spinners aside on the tailgate and rummaged through the loose stuff in the box until he found a bare hook—the kind you put bait on. He tied it to his line.

Now for some worms. Taking the shovel and one of the empty bean cans, he set out across the meadow, looking for a place free of undergrowth where he could start a hole. Seemed to be an open spot ahead. When he reached it, he stopped short!

Another digging. David stooped to examine the clods more closely. No way to tell what sort of tool had turned over the clumps so evenly, but this ground was fresh! Loose wet earth clung to the grass roots. They smelled muddy and green.

He straightened, shivering a little. The truck looked far away in the mist. All around him the meadow lay silent and smug with secrets. For a minute he stood there, scared. Tried to shrug it off. *Maybe I'll just use one of those spinners after all.*

David wouldn't let himself rush as he went back to the truck, but he was taut as wire inside. For a minute he stood looking at the junk on the tailgate, puzzled. Because he was sure he had left the spinners right there beside the fly box. Now—nothing. Except these pebbles, these two little round stones!

Picking one up, he turned it over. Just a plain old rock. But it hadn't been there before! In a sweep of panic he hurled it—far out into the river. It fell and was swallowed up. The water just kept flowing. Desperately he tried to calm down a little, laugh at it. Here he stood like a nut, with this other pebble clutched in his hand.

But I was in sight of the truck the whole time. Somebody would have had to crawl through the grass— He tried to picture it. Not the sort of thing his father would do, to play a silly trick like this. And yet the spinners couldn't have vanished all by themselves.

It occurred to him that a bold sort of kid would just find out what this was all about. Some loony old geezer slinking around the woods—somebody ought to see what he was up to. The thought made David's spine creep. Sissy . . . the old word slithered through his mind like a snake.

All right, I will! He put the fly box away in the camper, laid his rod inside, and closed the tailgate. Then hesitated, glancing downriver, but Mark was nowhere in sight. He probably wouldn't approve of this. *But if it hadn't been for me looking around, he wouldn't have known about the digging, even. And he seemed to think that was important.*

He felt a little steadier inside. It helped, too, to

have the fog lifting. Pale yellow light was eating through from the sun up there—a burning spot just above the rimrock. He could make out the faint profile of the towering cliff through the mist as it shifted and shredded.

Then, as he started across the meadow, a breeze began to stir and the vapors scattered fast. Coming to the old wagon road, David began to backtrack along it. That cabin his father had mentioned—that would be the place to start. But when he reached the woods he had to talk stiffly to himself to bolster his courage.

Nervous. You're always getting nervous. Don't be a dope. Big people never hurt kids—they can get sued or something. The most this old guy can do is yell at you. Besides he won't even see you if you don't make a whole lot of noise.

Overhead the sky was a vivid morning blue now. All around, the trees were still dripping, but sunlight glittered in every drop. Each time one fell it made a bright splash upon the silence. A giant dragonfly veered past David's head, darted into the woods and hung there, brilliant as a Christmas tree ornament. Motionless, it hovered right in front of a door-way. . . .

It was the cabin. In a little clearing the old place lay asleep under the soft fall of sunshine. Caved-in roof and a chimney still standing, but it had been a sturdy little hut once. The aged wooden beams had been shaped by an ax. The roof had been covered with sod—a little fresh green was starting up through the old matted dry grass that still clung to the timbers.

David walked over to it cautiously, but it was plain that no one had lived here in a long, long time. For a minute he stood listening, one hand warming on the sun-drenched wood of the doorway. A peaceful place—the whole flow of quiet years lay over this clearing. Nothing made a sound except the come-and-go breeze that stroked the pines.

And yet he was sure there was some other presence nearby in the forest. Just beyond here. Everything stood still inside him, he held his breath— and as the shuffling branches quieted he heard a faint, fretful little cry.

With an effort of will power, David made himself venture on deeper into the woods, keeping sight of the cabin over his shoulder from time to time. You could get turned around in this forest and never find your way out! He paused; the sound was hard to locate—a strange, breathless whining. He could have sworn it came from somewhere overhead. Even though it didn't make sense he kept looking up, half-expecting to see—

A face! There it was, peering down at him! With

48

a gasp he drew back. It almost seemed human—a dark face with big black eyes watching him through the crotch of a tree. Then it turned aside as if embarrassed to be discovered and he saw the long, furry muzzle and wet black nose. A bear cub!

As it let out another complaining little cry David began to laugh inside. He felt weak all over, laughing silently, warmly, in relief.

Clumsily the baby bear crawled through the crotch and sat there, an unhappy bunch of tawny fur with one foot dangling. Squirming, whimpering, it looked down at David, then up at something higher in the tree. Another one! The second cub was even lighter in color—almost silvery blond. It was far out on a branch, walking along unsteadily. David was afraid that at any minute it would come plunging down, but the cub's feet seemed to grip the tree bark like flypaper as it climbed down the trunk to join its brother. The two of them squeezed into the crotch together, squabbling, snapping at each other. As fidgety as two kids left on a park bench while their mama's gone shopping: "You stay right there and don't move until I get back."

How did she manage to tell them, though? And if they didn't mind, did they get licked? He glanced around, but there was no sign of the mother bear. Just as well, he supposed. She probably wouldn't understand that he liked those cubs. And it was possible that this was what Mark had in mind—the reason he had said to stick close to the truck.

It came over David that he'd been gone quite a while. The old fear stirred inside him as he remembered that this time he had really disobeyed instructions. And he didn't have much excuse. Mark was probably right about the bear doing that digging. As for the spinners—well, he hadn't solved that. Maybe the subject just wouldn't come up if he could get back there and get to fishing.

Hurrying, David took a short cut through the woods instead of following the twisted old track. As he went he snatched up a few sticks, with some notion of giving himself an alibi, just in case— Then as he came out into the open meadow above the camp, he saw that he was too late. Mark was already there, and—no doubt about it—he was mad.

Chapter 7

Mark was furious—the kind of anger that can burn like dry ice. "I assume you went quite a distance. You were gone long enough." His lips hardly moved.

"Just thought I'd get some wood," David mumbled.

Mark glanced at the fireplace. There was plenty of wood already stacked there. "I like to get the truth—" he began tersely.

"I wanted to go see the old man's cabin!"

"You recall, I told you to stick near the truck?"

"Yes, sir, but I thought—" David's throat was furry, he couldn't go on. It was a terrible look that Mark was giving him, like a judge.

Slowly Mark said, "If anything happened to you out here, with me, there'd be the devil to pay. I've undertaken a responsibility to see that no harm comes to you. Of course I assumed you'd been taught to obey. Here in this wild country you're not really old enough yet to decide for yourself what's safe and what isn't. So in the future will you kindly do as I ask? Oh, you don't have to fish if you have such a distaste for it. . . ."

David snatched up his rod and headed for the bank of the stream, his face flaming hot. Boiling with helpless resentment, he kicked over some of the rocks in the edge of the water. On the underside of one a crawly thing wriggled and tried to slither away. He grabbed it—it was squirmy in his fingers, but he was so worked up he hardly cared. Just jammed it onto the hook and threw the whole business into the water.

Fishing—what a bust! Supposed to be all this fun they talk about. Instead it's a—a—rotten test. He stood there, rigid with rebellion, until his fingers began to ache from gripping the rod so tightly. As he shifted hands, he jerked the rod—and froze. There was something on the end of his line. To make matters worse, he had hooked a fish.

With a confusion of emotions he stared at the ripples that fanned out in a V where his line cut the water. It must be a fairly little one, not to pull any harder than that. Not big enough to prove anything or show anybody—just a poor darn little fish that had been minding its own business. Now he was going to have to do something with it. If Mark didn't happen to notice, maybe he'd just get it off the hook somehow.

He was letting the automatic reel wind in, hanging onto the line with one hand so it wouldn't come too fast. When he had it almost to shore he felt it struggle a couple of times. Well, it was big enough to eat, he supposed miserably. At least a harsh man like Mark might think so. He could see it now, quivering down there in the shallows, a delicate sliver of life. David shuddered in sympathy with the trembling of that small fish.

When he heard his father coming, walking up through the grass, he tightened with defiance. *I won't, I won't kill it!* Never in his life had he hated anyone before as he hated Mark. So darn . . . darn . . . ready. And mean. Underneath you could feel the meanness about to come out. Brutal and everything. *Hit it on the head with a stick!*

What would a man like that do to you if you didn't obey him? Pick you up and chuck you into the water? The notion came whispering through his mind from deep in the past. Terror rose in David's throat as he stared at the current, swirling, slipping around the rocks, glossy as gray silk. He could almost feel strong hands gripping him, swinging him out over the small waves that sipped. . . .

As in a dream, David turned. The man loomed over him, fixing him with those fire-blue eyes. Blindly he threw down the rod and ran. Plunging, tripping over rocks, tearing loose from the stickly bushes that snatched at his legs—it was like the nightmares. He lunged on and on, the wind stinging his eyes to tears.

"David! David!" The voice haunted him. Mark was following, coming after him. *The gun—he's got a gun—!*

A sharp crack like a shot split the air and David went down. Flung himself forward into the meadow grass and tried to burrow under it. Then lay still. It was no use, the thud of feet was right on top of him.

"Are you hurt?" The hand that touched his shoulder was light. Then the grip grew firmer, making him sit up. "No, you're just—scared—stiff." Mark's face was grim with wonder.

David was staring at the gun, still in its holster. He heard himself say in a hoarse whisper, "There was a shot—"

"Was there?" Mark hunkered there beside him, eyes squinted beneath their brows. "Did you think somebody was shooting at you? Who?"

David was distantly surprised that he could still think. "The neighbor—you know, the old geezer." He pretended to look around for somebody else.

Dazed, he saw that they had come a long way up-stream. The truck was out of sight somewhere below. Here the river was different, frayed out into several channels that threaded through a flat willowy swamp.

"Have you got your breath?" Mark was helping him up. "Then come on. I'll show you what you heard." He led the way over to the nearest arm of the stream. It was clogged with dead brush which had dammed it so that the water had backed up into a big pool.

"Hear that?" Mark said softly. And David made out an odd chattering—it seemed to come from a pile of sticks heaped in the middle of the pond. "Beavers. The old lady's giving the kids their orders to stay close to the house. You frightened her," Mark added dryly. "That shot you heard was her tail smacking the water, warning the others to hit for home."

David stood, trying to take it in. Struggling to shake free of the lingering fear.

"You can figure it all out later," Mark said at last. "Right now we've got a fish to attend to."

"Yes, sir." David felt drained; there was no fight left in him.

Together they went back down the river. Back to the rod, still lying with its tip in the water. Faintly he hoped the little fish had somehow gotten off the

56

hook, but it hadn't. Just gone in close to the bank, trying to hide in the roots there.

Drawing it out of its shelter, pulling in line, Mark was talking to it in that curt, chopped-off way of his. "Got in trouble, eh? Didn't look that bait over very well, did you? And you not much bigger than it is. Maybe you learned enough to keep alive awhile."

Putting his hand in the water, he scooped up the small trout, holding it carefully. To David he went on, "A wet hand, and a loose grip—don't squeeze a fraction more than you have to, to hold on."

As gentle as a nurse picking a splinter, he backed the hook out of its mouth. Lowering the fish into a quiet spot in the water, he held it upright to help it get its balance. It hung there motionless as if it couldn't believe its good luck, then darted off in a spasm of freedom.

When Mark stood up, all the smile was gone from his face. He looked tired. "But what am I doing this for? To show off, maybe? I guess that's why I asked you out here. No reason why you should like to fish, or camp out, or anything else. I should never have begun this experiment. Of course I didn't dream you'd be so afraid of me. I'm sorry. Let's go home, David."

Part Two : THE NEIGHBOR

Chapter 8

David felt almost like that fish—as if a hook had been taken out of him. Walking along at Mark's elbow, heading for the truck, he went over it numbly: Nothing was going to happen. They were going home.

He was trying to get used to the idea when the breeze blew the piece of paper against his knees. Automatically he caught hold of it, wondering who had left loose trash lying around. It took him a minute to realize that it was their own grocery bag— all torn.

"Oh-oh." Mark eyed it a second, then swung around to look out across the quiet meadows. Nothing there. Abruptly he broke into a trot, heading for the truck. David began to hurry too, without knowing why.

When they reached the fire Mark paused. "I left the pan of bacon and eggs on that stone."

To one side they saw something black out in the grass—the frying pan, overturned and empty. David went to get it. As he followed Mark over to the pickup he saw more stuff scattered everywhere—broken eggshells, corn meal all over the ground. The bread wrapper was caught on a bush nearby, but the bread was gone. The box of sugar was split wide open. Mark walked over to rescue the coffee can which had spilled along with all the rest.

"My fault," he said irritably. "Should've known better than to leave things unwatched with a bear around." He began to gather up the bits of eggshell.

Privately David wished he could have watched that mama bear ripping into the groceries. After she'd had to eat old mice, the bacon and eggs must have tasted great. He could have used a big slather of bacon himself, now that they were going home.

"Do you reckon she left anything?" He began to kick through the grass around the truck.

Mark shook his head. "When they're hungry they'll sniff out every scrap of food you've got."

But maybe not that tin of meat in his overnight kit! David went to look in the truck, but the canvas bag was gone. Not under the bedroll or anywhere—

just vanished. Climbing down out of the pickup, he started off across the field, searching. The bear must have smelled the chocolate bar inside—probably took the bag off a little way to rip it open.

"Come back here, boy, unless you want to change your mind about climbing trees." Mark's tone was cross, but David didn't shrink under it as he had before. Strangely, he could understand; he always got cross too, when something was his fault.

Moseying back to his father's side, he remarked, "I don't see how it would help much to go up a tree. Bears learn that when they're just little."

"I'm not worried about a cub getting you," Mark said curtly.

"But can't big bears climb too?"

"Oh, they can. Yes." As he spoke Mark began to roll up their sleeping bags, pounding and pulling at them as if he really didn't want to do it. It was plain that he hated to have to leave this place. It seemed to take an effort for him to go on and answer David's question. "Except for grizzlies, all bears have the ability to climb. But they seldom go up a tree in pursuit of somebody. At any rate, it's all you can do—to try to get away from them."

"Why not grizzlies?" David asked, shivering—he'd read about grizzly bears somewhere, in a book. They were the most dangerous of all.

"Their claws are not sharp enough," Mark told him shortly.

"Oh." David was faintly disappointed.

"A grizzly can't retract its claws when it walks. A black bear can pull its claws in, just as a cat does—which keeps them sharp. The grizzly's claws stick out ahead of its foot all the time, so they're constantly being worn off on the ends. By the time it's grown, the grizzly gets too heavy for the blunt claws to support it. However, they can still rip open an elk with one swipe."

"I guess there aren't any grizzlies around here?"

"They keep to the high country. You'd find some up there." Mark glanced toward the cliff. As he stood for a minute, staring off at it, there was a look in his eyes—a distant look like a wish.

It made David uncomfortable for some reason. Grown people aren't supposed to care a whole lot about things. Not *that* much. He even felt a twinge of regret about having to leave this place himself, now that he wasn't so scared any more. The valley was warm and fresh-smelling under the sun. And it was an interesting thing, to have bears around—even just a black bear maybe. It occurred to him suddenly that the cubs had been light-colored.

"Do black bears ever have brown cubs?" he asked.

Mark was chucking the bedrolls into the back of

the pickup. "Of course. It's a general term, covers black, brown, cinnamon—Are you ready?"

"I can't find my overnight bag. I bet the bear got it." David began to poke around in the brush. Not thirty feet from the truck he came upon a small patch of wet earth with tracks leading across it. Squatting down for a better look, he made out the print of a broad heel and five big pads, and a couple of inches ahead of them, five gashes in the earth. David caught his breath hard. Because suddenly he knew something about this bear that Mark didn't.

Softly he asked, "What color is a grizzly?"

For a minute Mark didn't answer. He was just standing there by the tailgate, looking toward the river. At last he roused.

"What?"

"I just wondered—a grizzly bear is kind of brown, isn't it?"

"Their fur is dark at the roots, lighter on top. That's why they're called silvertip."

"And their faces are dark." David said it to himself. Mark didn't notice. He was still hesitating, staring out across the valley, short blond hair rumpled in the breeze and eyes deep in shadow.

In a burst of generosity David suggested, "Maybe we ought to stay here a little longer."

Mark shook his head. "When a thing's over, it's

over." But still he paused, looking around him like a man who's leaving a place and not coming back.

"Don't you think we ought to try to find my overnight kit?"

Mark brushed the question aside and went to get in the truck. Then stopping again, he glanced toward the river. All at once he walked to the front of the pickup and raised the hood. Taking off the radiator cap, he felt inside.

"We seemed to be heating up a little on the way over," he said. "I think I'd better put some water in."

David recognized that tone. It was the same one he used when he was making up a good excuse. And the way Mark went back and got out the coffee can and headed for the river—it struck an odd sympathy in him. Mark wanted to take just one more look at that water.

He slogged along through the grass with his shoulders sloping—David even knew that kind of walk. So many times he had scuffed along, wanting to kick something and bust it all to pieces. It came from being disappointed. David hated people who disappointed him. And suddenly he realized why he felt sort of guilty. Because this time he was the one who had made someone else feel that way.

As he turned it over in his mind David began to drift away from the truck.

66

Chapter 9

David hated to think he'd been stupid. But when he went back over it—the whole business of suspecting a plan, worrying that Mark would kill the little fish, running away, thinking somebody was shooting at him—it all seemed pretty dumb.

Mark—? He didn't know about Mark. And there wasn't going to be time to find out, now. For some reason, that made him feel worst of all. Because suppose . . .

Such an impossible idea stumbled into his mind that he couldn't seize it at once. His thoughts broke off short, and he looked around blankly as if this were some new place he was in. When his eye caught on something blue-and-white in the bushes, he stared at it a minute before he realized that it was his own pajama top!

Picking up the snagged garment, he examined it. Not much harm done. The bear must have dragged the kit clear over here to the edge of the woods, opened it up, and pulled the stuff out. David glanced around, thinking to see the bag itself close by, when something made him hold dead-still and listen. It was like a premonition of somebody hiding just around the corner. Under the straight-down noon heat the woods lay breathlessly quiet. Even the breeze had died. And yet leaves moved. That was what had warned him—a silent stirring, deep in the motionless forest.

Far back where the heavy shadow was crossed by thin shafts of sunlight, something walked. Bright speckles slipped and slid along a furry shoulder, a long curving back. David stood rooted. The rhythm of that silken stride reminded him of his dream last night, and he knew what it was that had stalked the meadow.

Oddly, he wasn't so frightened now. He just hoped the mother bear would come out in the open a minute so he could get a good look at her. She was far enough off that he didn't feel any special danger.

In a minute he caught another glimpse, of a heavy neck that thrust through the underbrush. She was moving at a long, swinging pace that would bring her out of the woods a hundred yards below him.

Abruptly it occurred to David that it would put her between him and the truck. He had wandered farther than he'd meant to.

Just to be on the safe side, he began to move cautiously toward the river, thinking to go in a wide circle that would get him back to the pickup without coming close to her. But it was too late. She was already there on the verge of the forest. Some instinct made him stand rigidly still as she raised a massive head, glossy with sunlight, and searched for scent upon the air.

At last, slowly she stepped out into the meadow. A huge bear—her fur had a dark undercast but the surface was pale as if it had been brushed with light frost. *Silvertip!* David wished Mark could see this. Risking a glance toward the truck, he saw his father there now, standing frozen beside the open hood, still holding the coffee can as if he had forgotten it. Even at this distance he looked tense as life-and-death.

David supposed she *was* dangerous. But still he wasn't too worried. She seemed so calm, her huge loose body covered with fur so thick you wanted to plunge your hands into it.

Now she settled back comfortably on her haunches, making a breathy noise, and at once the two cubs came scrambling through the grass to her side. Gathering them onto her lap like any mother, she let them nurse. As they squirmed and nuzzled her, they growled with pleasure, almost like the purring of cats. It made David want to wriggle, himself. For a minute he loved that bear! She was so big and soft, he wanted to throw his arms around her and rub his face against her velvety neck.

But Mark was making little short motions with his hand that meant "Find a tree and climb it." David began to edge off toward the forest a step at a time. Still not worried—it was plain she didn't see him. Besides, she was far enough away—closer to the truck than to him. At her slow gait it would take her a while to reach him if she did decide to.

Still, to be ready if he had to, he glanced over his shoulder, trying to spot a tree that looked possible to climb. The nearest ones were either too big or the limbs began too high off the ground. Farther on there was one with a low stub of a broken-off branch. As he sized it up, its needles began to shift in a slight current of wind that touched David's cheek, like an invisible hand, and went on to smooth down the meadow.

When it reached the bear her head came around cat-quick. In that split second David felt the first tremor of doubt. Sweeping the cubs from her, she reared, unfolding out of the deep grass to rise, taller and taller. Powerful front legs curved like a fighter's,

70

she stood, the great head swinging as she sniffed the air.

David knew the instant she saw him. She seemed to bristle with sudden fury. Unable to tear his look from her, he couldn't move. It was Mark's voice that jolted him loose.

"Run, David! Run!"

And he was running, the forest jarring in front of his eyes, his ears pounding—or was it her roar? It sounded close behind. David flung himself at the nearest tree and tried to scramble up it by sheer strength—couldn't get his knees around, just clung there stuck, a couple of feet off ground. A sharp sound cracked the silence—a shot. *Don't shoot her!* he screamed inside. And tore away from that tree to run on.

Blindly he pelted through brush, almost crashed into another tree—the one with the low stub of a limb. Up on it—leaped for the next branch and monkeyed his feet up over it fast. Hauled himself up lightly with a thin scorching strength he'd never known before.

"Higher!" Mark was yelling. "Go higher!"

In one swift glance David saw the grizzly coming by long leaps. Mark was running after her—he raised the gun to send another shot into the air.

David squirmed upward through a tangle of pine

71

boughs, skinned free of them and out onto a good sturdy limb—just in time. The tree shook violently, and he looked down into a terrible snarling face. Up she lunged, her long forelegs reaching as if they were hinged on with rubber. For one petrified instant he thought she was going to keep stretching. But the claws dug into the tree just inches below him. Mad black eyes glowered at him, then she grudgingly sank back onto all fours. In the bark of the tree there were white gashes.

"Are you all right?" Mark called in a strangled voice.

"Yeah," David yelled back.

And then his heart flipped over. She had turned with that awful quickness and was eying Mark. He had started to back up now—smoothly, half crouched, trying to look like part of the field. She let out a low bellow and moved after him. Mark began to hurry as she broke into a bounding gallop. Lifting the gun he fired one more shot in the air and ran.

The grizzly checked stride an instant, reared—then with another roar she broke into a dead run, lengthening out long and thin as a race horse. David clinched tight inside. Because Mark wasn't going to make it!

Chapter 10

Up in the tree David clung to his perch helplessly. He wanted to shut his eyes, but couldn't. Across the field the grizzly went with a wrenching speed that brought her closer to Mark with every leap. They were almost to the pickup, but there was no time to open the door. Flinging himself down headlong, he rolled under the truck just as she crashed into it.

For a minute she clawed the metal as if it were alive. Tore the side mirror off with one blow. Then dropping to all fours she began to circle, nosing beneath. She couldn't see under it too well on account of the deep grass, but she kept lunging out with one long arm like a cat trying to sweep a mouse out of its hiding place.

David broke out in a sweat. He could imagine

Mark rolling away from her, to this side and that, as she kept on pacing around the truck. Once she stopped restlessly to look toward the edge of the forest. Must be worried about the cubs. She started over that way, then some suspicion made her whirl and pounce back at the pickup with startling swiftness.

As she stalked around it, she was deadly quiet. Only let out a low growl once in a while, whenever she took a slash at Mark. Maybe—David shuddered—maybe she'd already got him. Maybe he was just lying there. Or else why didn't he shoot?

Now she was standing up to glare into the open engine. She must have seen Mark below on the ground, for the hair sprang up on her crest and she plunged a big front paw down past the motor. Snarling, she crammed her head and shoulders under the hood, trying to reach him.

Suddenly there came a sharp, crackling sound, a shower of sparks shot up out of the works. The grizzly leaped backward with a *whoof!* The ragged noise came again, more sparks, and she bolted. Galloping toward the forest, she must have called the cubs, for they rushed to her and all of them plunged into the deep undergrowth. There was a faint crashing, then everything was still.

David held his breath, waiting for her to come

back. But the meadow was quiet as a park. The only sound was the distant gurgle of the river. Worst of all, there was no sign of Mark. David wished he could get over there, though what he would find— Craning as far out as possible, he scanned the forest, but she was nowhere in sight. He had an idea, since she took the cubs with her, that she wouldn't be back, at least right now.

Cautiously David swung down out of the tree. Moving half crouched, close against the deep grass, he kept a sharp watch on the woods. When he was nearly to the pickup he straightened and ran the rest of the way. Now he could see the crushed front door where she had gone into it like a freight train. All over the side were long scratches that gleamed in the metal.

"Mark. *Mark!*" he yelled as he came up, and saw a stirring underneath. Awkwardly his father worked his way out. Lying on his back he inched his head and shoulders free, struggled up onto his elbows and pulled himself a little farther—enough to sit up. His clothes were torn, his face chalk-white.

"I wasn't sure she was gone." He looked around, blinking. "Couldn't see—" The way he sat, taking one deep breath after another, David sensed something.

"Are you okay?" he asked uncertainly.

77

Mark glanced down at the long scratch on his arm that showed through the torn sleeve of his shirt. "That was some scramble."

David crouched beside him, still wondering why he just sat there with his legs under the truck. "What happened? I saw a lot of sparks—"

"I cut the wire to the horn and shorted it out on the body of the truck. Made fireworks right in her face. I reckon—she'll tell her grandchildren about that one." Stiffly he began to drag himself out farther.

And David almost choked. Mark's left pants leg was ripped to shreds and bloody—blood all over his shoe. Through the matted sock it was welling up, streaming down bright red on the grass.

"She got a piece of me once," Mark began, then cut off short. "Good grief, boy, don't pass out! I'll need your help. Here—" he fumbled in his pocket and handed David a key. "In the strongbox you'll find some first-aid supplies."

In a glaze of shock David rushed around to the back of the camper and managed to get the chest unlocked. Under the ammunition and fishing stuff he found a box with medicines and clean rags in it.

"Bring a bottle of the drinking water, too," Mark called.

When he got back with everything David found that Mark had cut off the tattered Levis at the knee with his knife and had taken a strip from them to make a tourniquet around his leg. He was twisting it tight with a stick. "I hope she didn't cut a tendon," he muttered as he began to wash the blood off. "I can't move my foot much."

Even when he'd got the wound cleaned it looked terrible. Her claws had sunk into the muscle of his calf and raked downward—the whole ankle was a ragged mess. David had to swallow hard to keep his stomach in place, especially when Mark began to douse the raw flesh with antiseptic. As the sting of it got to him his hand started to shake. Handing the bottle to David he said, between clenched teeth, "You do it."

It took all David's gumption, but he poured the stuff on quickly just as Mark had done, until the whole wound had got some.

"Now make a pad out of those rags—that's the way—" Mark was trying to sound normal, but the words were strained.

"Does it hurt pretty much?" David asked shyly.

Mark took the bandage and pressed it to the torn leg, then began to fasten it on with adhesive tape. Around the calf, the ankle, then down under his instep and up and around again, as tight as he could make it.

"It needs some stitches, but this'll have to do for

now." Glancing up, he added, "This could have been you. If she hadn't checked stride when I fired that first shot in the air, you'd never have made that tree. That's what's got me unnerved."

In a clutch of remorse David blurted out honestly, "I know. It's all my fault! I shouldn't have gone so far, but I didn't know they could run that fast."

"That's finding out about bears the hard way, with her snapping at your rump." Mark's tight-drawn lips suddenly twisted in a short smile, enough to show that there were no hard feelings. "Lord, wasn't she beautiful, though? I'm glad I didn't have to shoot her."

"Were you going to?"

"I drew a bead on her as she was chasing you. It would have been risky—you were right in my line of fire. Then you were up and safe, thank God."

"But while she was clawing at you, why didn't you shoot her then?"

"A mother with cubs—?" Mark was cutting the ragged leather off his boot so that only the sole was left. He taped this onto the bottom of his foot and handed the roll of adhesive to David. "Put the box in the back of the truck again, but keep it handy. If"—he hesitated, then went on matter-of-factly—"if I should black out, don't get excited. Just hold that bottle of ammonia under my nose. Now give me a hand; let's see if I can stand on this."

The thought of Mark stretched out cold was so hard to imagine David tried not to think about it. Hurriedly he said, "Listen, maybe I could learn to drive so that you won't—"

But Mark was getting up, hanging hard onto the truck and gripping David's arm. "No use worrying about that yet." Stiffening with pain at every step, he made his way to the front of the car, but the effort seemed to sicken him. He hunched over with his elbows on the radiator. "I think—I—could use a pot of coffee."

"The coffee all got spilled. You know—"

"Oh. Yes. I forgot."

David was about to start for the ammonia, but Mark shook his head. Standing a little straighter, he leaned over to poke around the engine. For the first time it dawned on David that the bear might have hurt something in there. The air filter seemed to be a little smashed.

He touched it gingerly. "Do you reckon that's busted?"

"It's not serious. But the old gal sure made spaghetti out of the electrical system." Mark was staring down at a tangle of torn wires. "She got her claws hooked through 'em. When I startled her she almost took the whole works with her. Nope"—he let out a long unsteady sigh—"nobody's going to be driving for a while."

David's thoughts stretched off over the narrow trail that twisted away through miles and miles of woods to the nearest road. "Can you fix it?" he asked in a hush.

"Only the Lord knows."

And if not—? David couldn't ask that question.

"Funny"—Mark rubbed at his eyes as if they were hazy—"your mother was always worrying, always afraid some disaster would overtake us—off like this—in a lonesome spot. Something we couldn't get out of. It'd be a joke on me—if she turned out to be right."

Chapter 11

David wanted to go back to that tree again. It was as if there were some unfinished business there. He started to ask his father if it was O.K., but decided not to. Mark seemed to be feeling worse than he wanted to let on.

It was strange to think of anybody that strong being so shaken up. Of course anybody can get wounded, but somehow David couldn't have pictured his father acting just naturally, as if it hurt. He supposed by the time he got back Mark would be himself again—brisk, curt, and sure.

When he reached the trees, David hesitated, peering off into the deep stretches of the forest. But you could tell that the fearsome spell was over. The bushes were gossipy with birds and the squirrels busied about.

He ventured on until at last he stood under the

tree. When he looked up at the limb he'd been perched on, for the first time he realized how tall the grizzly was. It hardly seemed possible, and yet there were her claw marks, way high on the trunk! Stepping onto the broken stub, he jumped and caught the lowest branch. Just hung there a minute, thinking. It had been as if some juice had been turned on inside, to get him up there so fast. Of course, he *thought* he could do it again if he wanted to. But an hour ago he would have said he couldn't.

As he puzzled over it, something kept trying to elbow its way into his mind. That last-minute advice of his mother's about not doing things that are beyond your strength: "Just say no. Politely—no." To a grizzly? David grinned a little. But the smile faded into another more mysterious feeling.

Just as he had discovered something a while ago that Mark didn't know about the bear, now he was on the brink of some bigger secret. Something his mother didn't know. It set his heart pumping harder. A thing that had to be tested, though—he wished he could try it out. And all at once he knew how!

He was heading back to the truck at a trot when he stumbled onto his overnight kit. The green canvas bag was caught under a bush near where he had first found his pajamas. There was a slash in the side, but the rest of the contents hadn't been disturbed much. Of course the chocolate bar was gone. Didn't see the tin of meat, either. The bear surely wouldn't have known to take that. It should be where he had packed it, right here on top of his underwear. David dug around—nothing there. Nothing except— a small round pebble.

It gave him a start. Uneasily he glanced around, but the forest still sounded cheerful. Streamers of sunlight moved lazily as the branches stirred. Turning the stone over in his fingers David tried to think; then gave it up. There must be some good explanation, but he didn't have time to worry about it now. He had to start testing his discovery as soon as possible. Holding the torn kit so that the clothes wouldn't fall out, he went on toward the truck.

When he got there Mark was still pasty pale. As he worked, his face was slippery with sweat, although the day wasn't really that hot. Bending over the engine he was grumbling to himself. When he saw David he spoke irritably.

"Where've you been?"

"Just over to the woods for a minute. I found my bag."

"And risked your life again? Haven't you learned anything from all this?"

David had an impulse to let Mark in on just what he *had* learned, but his father didn't seem to be in a mood to listen. Maybe it would be better, he decided, to keep this a private thing.

"I'm sorry if I was gone too long," he said, subdued. "Did you need me to help you?"

"I need the Ford motor manual," Mark muttered, delving into the engine again. "Look under the front seat, if you will, and see whether you can find a roll of wire and some friction tape."

David went to put his kit away. He could imagine what Mark would say to some question about pebbles right now. Then going to dig around the junk on the floor of the truck he found the wire and something that looked like black adhesive tape.

"Is this it?" He took them to his father, who nodded vaguely.

"Do you want me for anything else?"

Mark began to peel the insulation back off the end of one of the broken connections with his knife.

"I mean," David went on carefully, "I thought maybe I ought to go fishing."

His father roused out of his concentration. "You thought what?"

"We're going to need something to eat."

"You stay right here!" Mark stared at him wide-eyed. "That's all we need, to have you get caught out again by that bear. *All we need!*"

David fell quiet. He'd thought that there were no

hard feelings, but he must have been mistaken. Mark looked up uncomfortably, fiddling with the tape. More quietly he said, "It's not your fault, David— none of this is. But if anything should threaten you now I couldn't do much about saving you. That grizzly could be back here any minute."

"I'd watch for her."

"What good would that do if she got between you and the truck?"

"Well, I could get down in the river. I can swim."

"So can she. For the love of Pete—!"

"I could float down and get to those reeds, and I'd pick one and duck under water and breathe through it. She couldn't even see me."

"That sounds like something out of a book."

David felt himself blushing. But who on earth would have guessed that a man like Mark would have read the Tarzan books, too? He stood awkwardly, watching for a while.

Finally, as if the silence were making him edgy, Mark paused in his work again. "I know, you're hungry. I can't do anything about that, either. But I guess I don't have any right to keep you from trying for food. Go on, then, but stay right by that big rock on the bank. If she shows up—well, you might not hear me call. I'll fire the gun. Don't waste time getting back."

Almost before the last word was out, David started off. He didn't blame Mark for being nervous; his foot was probably hurting something awful. And he looked as if he didn't know much about the wiring. Should have probably stayed around, David thought, to hand him tools and stuff. But food was important, too. And most of all he had to find out about himself before he went home.

As he headed for the river with the rod in his hand, he was thinking of his mother, how wonderful she was. He loved her more than ever, now that he realized there were things she didn't know—important things. Some day he'd explain them. It filled him with the tenderest sort of warmth.

And then he was at the edge of the stream, surveying the mysterious face of the water. He thought of the little fish and how he had dreaded to kill it. But that seemed a long way back in time, and mixed up with his blind rebellion against Mark. This was different—to stand here alone, knowing it was up to him to get them some food. It was like a law of nature—he knew what he must do. He just hoped that he could catch a good big one. He wasn't exactly sure how you go about being stronger than usual with a fly rod. But it would come. The surge of confidence excited him.

They needed a fish—and he was going to catch one.

Chapter 12

For a while David held the rod so strongly his hand ached. His eyes were strained from peering at the spot where his line disappeared into the swirling water. Everything in him leaned forward, tense. But nothing happened.

It occurred to him that his bait might be gone. He reeled in to look; the devil scratcher was still there, soggy, but wriggling. He let it back out again into the current. Poised, ready to jerk back at the first touch of a bite, he stood—it seemed like hours. And yet when he looked at the sun it hadn't dropped much in the sky.

Once he considered the possibility of wading just a little way into the stream. But that was out. All the bluff talk about swimming had been to impress

Mark. Actually the lapping of that water at his feet made David slightly sick. Anyhow, plenty of people catch fish from the bank. He tried to think how. Mostly they just sat there. But Mark had kept whipping his line back over his head and casting it so that the hook fell far out in the fast water. It seemed like a reasonable thing to try.

David flipped the rod, the line came flying out of the water right at him. The devil scratcher hit him smack in the face. Gave him such a spasm he almost lost his footing on the wet grass. When he'd got himself untangled he tried again more cautiously. The second cast was better, but as his hook arched out over the stream, the bait came off.

It wasn't easy to find another good big crawler. And then on the third cast he lost that one too. Worst of all, his discovery seemed to be ebbing away from him. He was beginning to feel small and narrow and worthless again, and he hated it.

One thing he was sure he remembered: Everything he had done right this morning, even the way he ran, had felt smooth. Now he knew he was being clumsy, so something had gone wrong. There must be some knack that you have to know about fishing before you can even use your extra strength on it. Much as he hated to bother Mark right now, he thought he'd better ask. This might be the last chance he would ever get to know whether he could or couldn't do a thing that he needed to do. If he really couldn't . . .

As David walked slowly back toward the truck he tried to drown out his disappointment with excuses. He reminded himself that even Mark hadn't caught a fish. But then that was exactly why David most wished he could have gotten one himself. Of course it really wasn't such a good time of day; early morning was best, Mark had said. *But there's just as many fish in there right now*, he told himself sternly, *and they ought to be able to see the bait better with the sun out*. Besides, if you're hungry, you don't feel like waiting until tomorrow morning.

And he was hungry. It came over him like a swarm of bees—he was awfully hungry! No food since last night; nothing but coffee this morning. This is what starving means, David thought with some alarm. He began to hurry.

Mark was nowhere in sight. Must be in the camper. As he came around back, he saw his father sprawled out on the floor of the truck bed. *But what's he doing?* David wondered. Looking for something? He lay crooked, one knee hitched up as if he had been crawling toward the first-aid box. The bandages on his foot were soaked through with blood.

"Mark?"

But the still figure didn't move.

Scrambling in, David bent over his father. He had never seen anybody unconscious before; he never dreamed how it took all the expression out of a face. Mark didn't look fierce any more. There were tired lines around his eyes and mouth. It was as if the life was draining out of him . . . .

In a panic David glanced at the injured foot. He had heard of people bleeding to death, but nobody ever said how long it took. He made himself break loose from the grip of alarm. Quickly he tore a strip off the edge of the ruined Levis, just as Mark had done, and tied it below the knee. There was a screwdriver on the floor—he thrust that through the knot and began to twist the cloth tighter until the skin pinched up. With one of the rags from the first-aid box he wrapped the whole thing around so it wouldn't unwind and loosen.

He remembered the ammonia, then, and uncorked it. But when he held it under Mark's nose nothing happened. Very cautiously he decided to turn his father's face a little so that he could hold the bottle closer. But when he touched that white cheek he gasped, to find it so clammy cold. In a rush David put a hand up under Mark's shirt, felt the slow, slow pump of a heartbeat. That was some relief, but the chill seemed to be all over his body. It was just common sense to try to get him warm.

Grabbing one of the rolled-up sleeping bags, David tore at the buckles to undo them. He shook the bedding out to full length; then, awkwardly, nervously, caught the limp figure under the arms and hauled it onto the mattress. He began to pile on blankets, every one they had. He was looking for more when he happened to glance at his father's face.

Mark's eyes were open. None too clear yet, but coming back. David never would have believed he could be that glad to have his father frown at him.

"What . . . ?" Mark wondered feebly. "I must've . . . funked out."

"Your foot's bleeding. I put the thing back on your leg." David tried to keep his voice from sounding shaky. "What else should I do?"

He could see Mark making an effort to think. "Go

out, scrape up all the coffee you can find . . . don't worry if there's dirt . . . boil some strong. . . ."

"How about your foot?"

"It can wait."

"But—" Dirty coffee seemed such a poor remedy for anything.

"Please, David . . . " Mark closed his eyes again.

The sun was behind the mountains, twilight settling in fast, when David jumped down out of the truck. The great cliff was golden with light—a softer brilliance than yesterday. And the evening was warmer—the wind was coming up the valley now, out of the south.

It helped steady him to breathe this calm air without the sun battering down all over everything. It helped him face the quiet, dreadful reality—that they were in serious trouble now. Miles from nowhere, car conked out, no food. And Mark so far gone he was out of his head. Must be, if all he could think of was a cup of coffee!

Chapter 13

It was muddy coffee and there were bits of grass in it.
Hardly a thing to give a sick man. But it was bubbling hot—that at least ought to help.

When David brought it to his father's side Mark
made an effort to hitch up onto his elbows. David
screwed up his nerve to try to help. *Easy—slide an
arm under his shoulders—yeah, like that*—Mark drank
some of the stuff, choking on it a little. David tried
to hold the cup steady. Self-conscious, awed by the
hard muscle that leaned against his puny support, he
wondered what he'd better do next.

The real problem was the torn ankle. Ought to
take the old bandages off and put new ones on.
Mother said you should keep a cut good and clean.
It wasn't going to be a nice job—they were all stuck

96

together. Letting Mark lie back on the bedding, David went to dig out the electric lantern. It was getting gloomy in the camper. When he found the switch, and pale metallic light shot out into the corners, David felt a little firmer. Just about able to tackle his job.

"About your foot—" he began.

Mark stirred feebly. "I can't feel it at all—should be hurting like blazes. Better take the tourniquet off."

David stared at him aghast. His father obviously had no idea what he was saying.

"Well, boy . . . go on . . . "

"Yes, sir. Only you don't know—I mean, it was bleeding pretty badly."

"Then get a pillow."

Which was all right, but it didn't solve anything. David brought one and went to raise his father's head.

"No, no," Mark muttered vaguely. "The feet . . . under the feet . . . "

Now he was really delirious. It was plain that the coffee had done him no good. And he was asking for more.

"Better give me another shot of that coffee."

Desperately David searched for a way to refuse. "Mother says it's not good for a person."

Mark's eyes flared wide. "Who's calling the turn here, anyhow?"

David swallowed hard, trying to sound respectful. "You aren't very well, sir, and—and—"

"And you think you know best?" Angrily Mark started to sit up but couldn't make it. Helpless, he lay staring at the roof of the camper. "I guess," he said faintly, "I'm in no position to argue. If you want to take over, go ahead."

It disturbed David a little. He really didn't have much to go ahead on. Just thought he'd bandage that foot again. He went to open the first-aid box.

"One thing . . ." Behind him Mark spoke in a remote voice as if he were drifting off to sleep. "That generator . . . I doubt if you could rewire it."

David looked over his shoulder, startled. But his father's face had no hint of humor in it as he went on. "So my advice . . . for what it's worth . . . is that you start walking out of here, come daylight. Take the gun. Twelve miles of forest . . . could be dangerous."

"And what would you do?" David burst out.

"By then it won't matter." There was no emotion at all in the slow words. "If you take the bandages off now . . . open up the wound again . . . I'll lose some more blood. Maybe too much. Of course, there's the tourniquet. But if you leave that on, gangrene will set in. Flesh rots . . . . Anyhow, if I don't get another shot of hot coffee I may not pull out of this shock. That'll be that." He stared up at the ceiling.

David felt embarrassment break out all over him in prickles. With clumsy haste he untied the tourniquet, lifted the injured ankle onto the pillow.

"Both feet," Mark said remotely. "Raise 'em both."

David obeyed without a word, then picked up the coffee pot. "I'd better heat it again," he mumbled and rushed out into the darkness.

It's what you get, he accused himself, *for trying to be responsible and think and all—you end up acting like a dope.* And the confident feeling, that was just a silly idea too. *You're nothing but a dumb kid— that's what Mark is thinking right now!* Coffee sizzled up the spout and boiled over.

When David climbed back into the truck again, he'd have given anything not to have to touch his father. But he braced Mark's shoulders and helped him drink—swallow by swallow, downing the hot brew as if it were medicine.

"Tastes foul, but it's taking hold," Mark said doggedly. "Let's have some more."

Silently David poured out another cupful. And this time he could feel the warmth begin to spread back into that lanky frame propped against him.

Mark seemed to be pulling himself together by sheer will power. Secretly David had to admit a respect for anybody who could revive by pure stubbornness.

I should have had enough sense, he told himself scornfully, *to guess that Mark knew what he was doing, even flat on his back.*

As he lay there now, he was getting some color again. His eyes were in better focus—studying David.

Go on, then, and bawl me out. I guess I got out of line. Only if you just knew—I really did think you were out of your head.

At last Mark said, "Thanks." Then he repeated it. "Thank you, for helping out so quickly. When a person's in shock—actually it's like a cramp. Your whole body's constricted, you don't get enough circulation. Best remedy is a stimulant. Hot tea or coffee. And plenty of blankets. That was good thinking, to cover me up."

It was nice of him. It was O.K. He wasn't going to rub it in. Even trying to explain things. David appreciated that. Taking a deep breath he said, "I'm sorry I tried to—I mean, I'm sorry I didn't do—"

Mark made a little gesture that meant "forget it."

"I didn't catch any fish, either," David blundered on, bound to get his shame out of his system. "I thought I—I mean, I know I should have asked you how."

It was almost a laugh, the little snort Mark made. "Don't know why you should put any special faith in what I say. I couldn't even keep a bear from stealing our bacon." After a minute he went on. "This whole business has turned out to be a pain in the neck, and a good deal of it is my fault. Never figured it could happen to me. When you've been used to counting on your muscle, you assume that if you ever get hurt you'll just keep going somehow, like the heroes on TV, staggering along, pretending it doesn't bother you much. It's pretty unsettling to find out, when the time comes, that you can't. A while ago I barely had enough sense left to lie down before I fell down."

This was just another way of trying to square things between them, David knew. He even had an impulse to say something friendly in return.

"I reckon you'll feel better tomorrow—" But it came out more like a question.

"I've darn well got to," Mark said painfully. "It's going to take all we both can do—to get out of this spot."

Again David recognized a generous gesture, Mark trying to make him a partner in the business. Out of the shadows he watched the man, this stranger he had driven off with yesterday. Still something giant about him, like the brooding figure of the nightmares, only laid out helpless in the lantern light. Not so ready any more—

But he'd been good and ready when the grizzly was attacking. David glanced at the dark spot that was coming through the blanket where it covered Mark's torn foot. Ready to get himself killed. And all for me—? The confusion inside him began to tighten into an answer. It was coming back to him, the way Mark had said yesterday:

"When a man has a son . . ."

Chapter 14

Through the window of the camper David watched the night sky turn radiant behind the cliff. Moon must be rising, spreading light ahead of it. Up there on the rim of rock a lone pine tree stood black against the growing brilliance. All around it the glow was like a heavy fall of rain, drenching the tree, swallowing it up. And then there was a piece of the moon itself, burning like a bubble of white fire. It swelled, bigger and bigger, until it burst free, and rose. It was as if the rock hung back, the earth below crouched down while the moon lifted, flooding the valley with light.

David let his breath out quietly so that his father wouldn't hear. He was pretty sure that Mark was asleep. Lying wide-eyed in the warm night, David thought of all the people out there in the distant stretches of the world—asleep. He wondered how they could drift off, just forget all the things that needed to be thought about. He couldn't.

As a matter of fact, he thought *somebody* ought to stay awake and keep watch. It was one thing he could do—stand guard so Mark could get some rest. Taut as wire he lay and listened. The other part of his mind was reaching.

He kept living over that few minutes when the grizzly had been after him. Not like a nightmare— what came back clearest was the excitement of being beyond her reach, just above the snarling jaws. Now thinking of it all again and considering the jam they were in, still he was glad it had happened. The most amazing thing that ever *had* happened. Even Mark, hurt as he was, had marveled over it. He'd said she was beautiful. And for a minute there, as they had crouched together beside the truck, it had been almost as if the two of them were friends—kids having the same shudders of relief and wonder.

David wondered where the grizzly was now—probably asleep like everybody else. He could picture her all curled up somewhere with the cubs tucked under the folds of her fur.

It made him remember how, when he was younger, his own mother used to take him into her bed after he'd had one of the bad dreams. It had always been

104

one of his warmest memories. Now, though—right now when he was lying here, keeping watch all by himself—it made him sheepish to recall those baby days. He tried to shove the thought out of his mind. But it left him more lonely than ever in his life. As confused as if he'd suddenly got separated from his mother in a crowd.

Separated from the whole crazy darn world. Everybody else goes around grinning, all happy that they made the team at school. They wouldn't know what to do with a grizzly if they ever did see one. All most people do is just eat and play, and at night they go off to sleep. . . .

A faint sound brought David alert. Far away, high on the air, it came fitfully like the baying of a pack of ghost dogs racing down the sky. A shiver ran along his spine.

And out of the darkness Mark spoke softly. "That's an eerie cry—always makes me restless."

"What is it?" David asked in a hush.

"Wild geese. Heading north."

For a minute they lay until the distant cry of the honkers had faded. Some of the tightness unraveled in David. It wasn't a bad feeling, to discover that Mark was lying here awake, too. Even thinking the same kind of thing. Sharing a far-off rush of wings.

"Proud, lonesome birds," Mark went on distantly.

"Driving head-on into cold skies to get as far from civilization as they can, to bring up their young in a secret place. I always envied them." Then he stirred and sighed. "Maybe that's what's wrong with me."

David didn't understand. He was still picturing the secret little lake somewhere deep in the northern forests where the geese could swim just quietly.

Mark was rambling on in a feverish voice. "I've sometimes been looked upon as a screwball, for wanting to get off by myself. Never cared much what other people thought. Now I wonder." He sounded sort of bitter. "Any other father is glad enough to sit around the house, read the sports pages on a Sunday. Take a nap. Go for a picnic in the park."

David thought of the time he and his mother had taken a drive one Sunday. They had eaten chicken sandwiches at a roadside rest. It had been nice of her to plan it. But it wasn't a whole barrel of fun. She hadn't liked it much, either—there'd been a lot of trash that other people had thrown around.

"And afterward," Mark was going on unhappily, "they play badminton. Don't they? Isn't that what a kid pictures for a father—some guy who'll wash the car in summer and shovel sidewalks in winter? And never get you into any tight corners?"

David didn't know how to answer. It was true, and yet—not just the way Mark was putting it, like

106

some sort of blame on himself. For lack of a reply, he blurted out a question.

"What did your dad do?"

Mark went dead quiet. David couldn't even hear him breathing for a minute. "My father?" he said at last, trying to make it sound careless. "I grew up on a ranch. Money was short; there was no time for anything but work. Pa was a hard-handed man. I learned a lot from him—especially how to duck."

"He—licked you?"

"Did he! I remember once when I'd just gotten thrown twice by a roan colt. It was a mean horse. I couldn't see much point getting on it again." Mark laughed, but you could tell it wasn't really funny, remembering. "Pa took a length of hose and got on that horse, beat the tar out of it, rode it to a flat-footed standstill. Then he got off and whaled me with the same piece of hose. Couldn't lie on my back for a week."

David wriggled over onto his belly uncomfortably. But then he had heard grownups do this, talk about the whippings they got when they were kids, as if it were the best thing on earth that could happen. They'd always finish by saying, "Yes, sir, my folks raised me right," or something like that.

"You think that's right?" he asked with his face half muffled in the bedding.

When he answered Mark sounded faraway, back in years long ago. "When I was young, I was afraid of Pa. I knew there was no kindness in him. Later on I plain hated him for what he'd done to my mother."

"Did he hit her, too?"

"No. She never gave him an argument. I never heard her say more than a few words at a time. After years of his bullying she wasn't even a person."

David thought Mark's foot must be getting worse. There was a ring of pain in the words, spoken so harshly out of the darkness.

"When I was sixteen," he went on, "she died. I left home the next day, never went back. It wasn't the kind of childhood you think about with pleasure. But I did think it was a lesson, of sorts. I swore no kid of mine would ever be afraid of me. How wrong could I get?" Even after he stopped talking the words echoed in the nearness of the camper.

As they lay in that pulsing silence, David wanted to cry out in protest. *Listen, I know badminton's a silly game! I never wanted to do stuff like that!* He was just shaping up words to say it out loud when his attention snagged. A current of south wind was eddying through the truck, smelling of new grass and spring leaves. A soft breeze, and yet all at once it made his heart start kicking against his ribs. He made a move to scramble up in a hurry, but Mark's hand touched his shoulder in the dark.

"Easy," he whispered. So he had sensed it, too.

Cautiously they laid back their blankets and sat up. At first glance the meadow looked deserted under the torrent of moonlight. Nothing cast a shadow except that mound of rock—and then David froze. There'd been no huge jagged stone out there before! Peering hard, he made out the silhouette of a long back, curving up to a great hump of a shoulder from which neck and head thrust forward.

"It's her!" he breathed.

"No! Too big. That's the old man." Mark was fumbling for something under the blankets. David heard a little click and glanced over his shoulder to catch a glint of light off metal. His father was checking the .357 Magnum. Speaking very softly into David's ear, he said, "If he gets the scent of blood, he could smash his way in here. If he tries, keep behind me. He'll be tough to stop, even with this."

The grizzly was coming toward them at a slow walk, all moving light and shadows. Nearer and nearer, nosing the air. David could see now that this one had a longer stride, more powerful haunches. The heavy mass of shoulder fur rippled in the moonlight. When the bear was only fifty feet from the truck, it paused and looked sharply toward the woods.

Half rising on its hind legs, it stood like a giant sculpture edged in silver.

And then they saw, too—a second furry shape starting out of the shadow of the forest.

"Is it her?" David whispered.

"Must be. She'd never let another bear stay around these parts—not with those cubs. She won't even welcome the old man." Mark fell silent, watching.

The grizzlies moved toward each other warily. Over the meadow lay that awful hush, as if even little creatures in the grass must crouch, afraid to move. On the shifting breeze came a low whining, growling sound as the bears seemed to bicker across twenty feet of space. The male took one more step— and she leaped, like a spring uncoiling.

They grappled in a terrible clutch of mingled snarls and snapping jaws. Two monstrous shadowy hulks that reared and wrestled and bit in a swift battle across the field. Once they came straight at the truck —Mark gripped David's arm, ready to yank him back. But they veered past.

Furiously the mother grizzly drove the male away— he yielded a few steps, a few more. Then wheeled and lumbered off a hundred feet. For a minute the two of them stood off from each other. Sullenly he licked at his shoulder, then moved on down the valley.

For a time she watched after him. Finally, as if

112

satisfied that he was gone, she stalked back into the shadows of the forest.

Mark drew a long breath. "That was close." He found the lantern and switched it on.

David was chattering with excitement. "Could he really have gotten in here?"

"That bear could crumple this light aluminum like tinfoil." Mark sank back onto his bedding. When he lit a cigarette his hands weren't too steady.

Still flushed with the wonder of the fight, David said, "But why was she so mean to him?"

"Protecting the cubs. Not all animals are born to be good fathers." Mark had a strange look in his eyes. Some trick of the lantern light made them look bright-hot. "The male grizzly is apt to hurt his own young. She always drives him off—wonderful, un-failing instinct."

"Yeah?" Then some undertone got through to David and he quieted, uneasily.

Mark was going on in that disconnected way. "These wilds . . . one reason I come out here—they give you clearer air, you see things that you couldn't before. All my life I've taken risks, maybe worse ones than I thought. Whenever I'd read about some-body being hurt or killed I always figured they must have been careless. Or foolish. Now I'd be inclined to give 'em the benefit of a doubt. Oh, I'd still take the chance. To me it's worth it. But to put you in such danger—I should have my head examined!"

But I don't mind! David shouted inside. *It's all right, it's good. There aren't many people who ever get to see grizzlies fight!* Yet he couldn't get it out—not after that awful time this morning. How could he explain that so much had changed since then?

Mark was eying him wearily. "Don't be too upset, David. Try to get some sleep. He won't be back tonight. In fact, if he has any sense"—Mark crushed out his cigarette angrily—"he'll head for the high lonesome country and stay there."

But long after the lantern was turned off, David lay thinking about those last words. Because Mark hadn't just been talking about a bear.

Part Three : HUNGER

Chapter 15

Sitting on the big rock, legs a-dangle, line trailing off downstream, David stared into the swirling dark waters. That deep dread was still there; it hadn't changed. It steadied him to recognize the familiar fear. So much else had turned upside down in his mind.

This place, this valley with gray dawn spreading over it—the deserted valley that he'd hated so much just night before last—now it was part of him, like a wish. It was as if he had lived his whole life here and soon would have to leave it, never see it again. He'd forget what it looked like. Back there in town, with people around and teachers asking their questions and cars honking, he'd lose this valley!

Fervently David began to memorize: the cool sweep of grassland with the rough-and-tumble river playing through it, the forest on every side, and the cliff over there shouldering up against the glow of the rising sun. That pine tree, hanging crooked, pointing the way to the wild country beyond—his wish stretched out toward that.

His look jogged downward to the sloping skirt at the bottom of the rock face. He had caught a glimpse of something moving in the heavy shadows there. Searching intently, he found it again—a big animal of some kind, climbing upward among the sparse trees, toward a crevice in the rocks. Another thing to hold on to, after this is over—to remember how it was, to know that a wild thing is out there roaming free and dangerous. From time to time in between watching his line he followed the slow progress of the creature.

The sun came up almost suddenly. Breaking onto the hushed world below, it struck golden sparks off the river. Where the water dashed over a boulder, the light made a little rainbow only a couple of feet across. David wished he could tell all this to somebody—not any of the guys at school, they'd snicker. Mother wouldn't. Of course he doubted if she'd care much for really wild beasts, though she was a good sport about tadpoles and had said he could raise a hamster this summer.

When he looked next time, the animal was higher on the slope. It came out into the sunshine for a minute and David saw that it was the grizzly—the big male. Even at that distance you couldn't mistake the heavy shag of fur around its shoulders or the majestic stride. It was making its way up toward the wilderness, alone, just as Mark had predicted.

The vague wish swelled inside of David, filled him with some wordless longing that followed the bear as it moved into the shadows and was gone. His glance strayed toward the pickup where Mark bent over the motor, and the wish leaped in that direction. Pretty soon his father would be gone, too— The fullness collapsed, leaving David all caved in. *I'm just hungry*, he thought weakly, churning with emptiness.

And Mark must feel even worse. He'd hardly slept at all. All night he had kept moving, easing his foot this way and that. This morning there were haggard lines around his mouth and his eyes were quiet and tired. The zest was gone from his face; for some reason he hadn't wanted to talk about the fishing. Just said, "Stick with the bait and stay close by." Then he'd gone to work on the truck.

Mark was blaming himself for everything, David thought, with a sharp twinge of sympathy. The food, the bear, especially for not being too good at fixing the car. And a lot else. The way he had talked of his own father last night—he was comparing himself to this other man who had no kindness. It wasn't

true, either; Mark wasn't unkind at all. Look at
how he'd let the little fish go. And he wouldn't shoot
the mother bear, even to save his own life. All the
same, he was blaming himself because he thought
David was still frightened of him, since that awful
few minutes yesterday morning.

And it seemed so silly now, to have run away like
that. David wished he could walk up and say right
out, "I'm not scared of you, Mark, honest." But he
couldn't. And yet he didn't want his father to go
back to Africa thinking such a thing.

Because that was one fact he was sure of—Mark
had decided to go away for good. You could tell
it in the way he talked, everything sounded like "good-
by." David could even understand that, in a way,
because he'd wanted to just vanish too, sometimes,
when he had made a mess of things.

And this trip was a real bust of a mess. They
weren't out of it yet, either. So it was strange how
peaceful it seemed, to be sitting here on the rock.
When he thought back over all the other Sunday
mornings—lying around the apartment, reading
Prince Valiant and watching a couple of TV shows,
playing "concentration" with Mother—they were so
tame he'd never even worked up an appetite. When
he thought of all the times he'd eaten a big dinner
that he didn't want . . .

120

Delicately he jerked his line, but there was nothing on it. If he could just catch a fish and give it to Mark, maybe somehow that would help set things straight between them. Troubled, he glanced toward the truck again.

Mark was looking over at the forest, must have seen something. He turned to motion to David with a long sweep of his arm. It meant *hurry!*

The rod—no, leave the rod! David stuck it in a bush and rushed up the bank. Even as he ran toward his father he was thinking, *I've got to remember this, too.*

By the time he reached the pickup Mark had the door open. Together they crowded into the front seat.

"She's up there," Mark was saying. "No close call this time, but it's best to be on the safe side."

Then David saw her too. She had come out of the woods a good way up the valley, the cubs at her side. All three of them were moving at a steady pace, heading for the stream. As Mark watched her go, his stern face took on a hint of that keenness again.

"Could be this place has gotten too crowded for her."

"You were right about the other one," David told him. "I saw it way up on the side of the cliff over there."

For a minute things were close and warm between

them as they watched the mother grizzly step down to the river's edge and walk on in.

"How will the cubs get across?" David asked.

"Most animals can swim as soon as they can walk. It comes to them naturally."

Now the first cub plunged into the water, paddling out into the current, riding the ripples like a furry cork. The other fretted along the shore. For a minute the mother seemed to be calling to it. Finally she went back. The cub scrambled up onto her, clinging to the silvery fur as she struck out across the river.

"A fine instinct," Mark said thoughtfully. "A doggone fine mother."

On the opposite bank she shook, spraying water like a dog, while the cub ran to catch up with the other. Then the three of them moved on across the open meadow into the trees on the far side of the valley. David was sorry to see her go. He thought Mark was too.

But his father said, "Now I won't worry about you so much." Mark's face was drawn again as he started to open the door of the truck.

David wished he could hold on to the minute of friendliness. There were some things he really wanted to ask Mark. "I'm not getting any bites," he said tentatively. "What should I do?"

"Put on a spinner, maybe."

122

"I'd rather try flies, if you'd tell me how."

Mark gave him a puzzled look. Then his face toughened and he said, "It would take more than one lesson."

"I saw some bugs out there hopping around on the water."

Mark shrugged. "Go ahead, try anything you want to. Nobody should tell somebody else what to fish with."

"I lost the spinners!" David blurted out. "Yesterday."

"Oh." For a minute Mark's face seemed about to twitch free of its moody look.

And someday, David promised privately, *I'll tell you about the whole crazy thing*. Except there wasn't going to be any "someday." In a kind of anguish he said, "You wanted to teach me the flies when we first came here."

"That was a long way back," Mark said distantly. "There's no time now. But if you want to fool around with it, take my hat. I put a good selection of flies in the band. If one doesn't work, try another." The instructions seemed to come hard, as if he were talking against his will about something very important. "Keep your fly moving on the surface of the water. Try not to cast in the same place twice. Walk downstream as you fish, but don't go too far.

When you reach that clump of willows come back and work this stretch over again."

He climbed out of the car, careful of the damaged foot. He had made a crude brace of sticks to take some of the weight when he had to step on it. Even so, there was fresh blood coming through the old brown stains.

"Maybe I ought to stay and help you?" David offered.

Roughly Mark said, "I'm all right. I may have a touch of fever, but it won't knock me out again, if that's what you're afraid of."

David felt a flood of heat to his face, as if he had been accused. "I'm not afraid," he said with as much dignity as he could. He went to the rear of the truck and found the fishing hat. When he came back around front, it was Mark who looked flustered.

"I may need you later," he said, in a tone of apology. "Meanwhile, about casting—use more wrist action than you were doing yesterday. Let the rod do the work." With a screwdriver he made a smooth forward-and-backward stroke. "There's a rhythm to it. A nice, easy . . . " He sighed and tossed the tool aside. "One more thing. The best place to set your fly down is on the opposite side of the current. Sometimes you can't reach it unless you wade out."

Here it came, and David hadn't even thought of

a good excuse yet to get out of it! Right now, too, when he was wishing things wouldn't be so touchy between them.

"You'll have to wade a stream sooner or later if you ever want to be a fly fisherman. Which is up to you. Someday you'll decide. For right now"— Mark was looking off upstream, where the bears had disappeared—"I want you to stay on dry ground. I know, it sounds unreasonable, but I'll have to ask you to do as I say. Fish or no fish, don't set foot in the water." And there was no doubt about it: That was an order.

Chapter 16

Mark's hat felt strange. David kept reaching up to make sure it was cocked right. A good hat. With the kind of brim that slants over one eye—except that David couldn't wear it that way. It settled too far down on his ears. So he wore it shoved back on his head and it almost fit.

There must have been fifteen flies stuck in the band. By now he had tried almost all of them. Gray ones. Brown fuzzy ones. For an hour or more he had been casting until his arm and wrist ached. The truth was, he didn't really believe he was going to catch a fish.

Neither did Mark. Wouldn't even begin to teach

him the real tricks of it. And acting so odd about not going in the water—it was plain that he had written David off as a weakling. A mama's kid, just like the little sissy bear cub that couldn't swim the river.

David eyed the stream angrily. It really wasn't all that dangerous. Right here, for instance, there was a clean, sloping gravel bottom. The water wasn't more than a foot deep—you could see every pebble. It even looked fairly inviting, what with the sun beating down so hot.

Must be about lunchtime. Right now, David thought, he would have given anything on earth—anything—to be able to walk up to Mark with a trout in his hand, a good one. To say carelessly, "Reckon you're pretty hungry. Shall I build a fire?"

Not that it was so brave, catching a fish. But it would prove he wasn't just a dope or something. It might even jolt Mark into listening to some good straight talk. Though what David would say if he did have the chance— He couldn't even plan it.

So just think about fishing. If the fool trout don't like crawlers or these flies, then what do they want? He had reached the clump of willows where he was supposed to turn back. As he stood there, cudgeling his brain for some clue, he heard a small splash far beneath the overhanging willow branches. They were the first things beginning to turn green—a nice spot for a fish to hide under. Couldn't see anything in the water, but crawling up one of the shoots was a bug. He made a grab—it flew. And as it rose in the sunlight he was struck by the color: pink, with a fuzz of brown around it.

Searching the willows, he found another one, a pale pink insect with brown wings. Seizing it, he held it clenched in one hand as he started for the pickup at a trot. Better not waste time; it looked as though it might rain. Up between the high peaks at the north end of the valley a big cloud was beginning to bulge against the sky. White and beautiful, but it was a thunderhead just the same.

Mark was aware of it too. He glanced up that way, then tackled his work harder than ever. Didn't even pause as David came up.

"I'm not having much luck, sir." He tried to make it sound offhand. "I was wondering, there's a place I could go out in the stream just a little way—"

"No!" Mark sort of exploded down there in the depths of the engine. Hot and flushed, with a blond stubble of beard on his cheeks, he looked upset as he glared at the mixture of wires. "Since you're here,

you might help me. Get in the front seat and turn the key when I tell you."

David put the dead bug in his pocket. If there was one thing he had learned, it was never to bother grownups with your own problems when they're busy. He stepped up into the driver's seat.

"All right . . . now."

But when he switched the key, nothing happened. "Again."

The motor was dead as a chunk of scrap metal. Funny how it takes one little thing to bring it to life and make it work. David sat, stuck and stumped, watching the thunderhead build higher and higher into the sky.

He hoped it wasn't stormy down in the city. His mother didn't like lightning. Girls never do. A wave of fondness for her swept through him, filling the hollowness for a minute. If Mark only knew how nice she had been all these years, trying to fix the bike when it got broken. And getting that book on how to find gold, just because David had asked a few questions. She was always baking cookies, too— he really liked to come home after school. She didn't tell him he must. In fact she was awfully sorry he didn't make the baseball team.

In the big silence inside him he told it all to Mark. *And if girls get jittery about bears and stuff, you've just got to be kind. Don't get mad at them for being nervous. That's why they need men around all the time. You should have seen how she looked, all excited, Friday when we were waiting for you. I think she wanted you to come!*

Something began to hum inside him, a current of purpose that almost made him wriggle. To do something about it all— *I've got to do something!* Not just a wish any more, but a desperation. Climbing down out of the pickup, he went to stand beside his father.

"See that?" Mark held up an end of wire. "It goes to the solenoid. It should be the connection to the starter. But it doesn't work."

Nobody had ever talked to David about solenoids. It gave him a jolt of strength to go ahead. "I wish I knew about cars," he said, speaking fast and recklessly. "We had an awful time last fall when the tire went flat. Mother didn't know how to work the jack. Of course we figured it out, but she broke her fingernail and got grease all over her dress."

Mark scowled at the wire he was splicing. "Hand me the tape, will you?"

"She has to do a lot of hard things at home, too. Last week we had a thunderstorm and the lights went out. She had to change the fuse in the dark—it was kind of scary."

"David, will you please try the ignition again?" Mark sounded tormented.

Reaching into the front seat, David turned the key. No luck. "We never did know why the fuse blew out, either."

"Probably turned too many lights on at once. She used to do that when a storm hit." For a second Mark's voice softened. Then he said gruffly, "Don't worry. That thunderhead up there is local. Weather's probably all right back in town."

"It isn't only lightning; it's a lot of things. I mean—she's a girl and they get scared. She tries not to let on—"

Mark looked up as if that surprised him. "She must have changed," he muttered, almost to himself. "But then, who hasn't—all these years—"

David was rushing on. "She talks a lot when she's nervous. Only now there isn't anybody at home for her to talk to."

"And if I don't get this truck in shape soon, there won't be anybody there by seven tonight—which is when I promised to have you back. Will you try that switch again?"

So that was why Mark was working so furiously. And why he was so irritated. Because they had to get back by a certain time. When the motor didn't turn over he cussed under his breath. David shuddered when he thought how there was going to be this terrible fight when they did get home. The worst thing that could happen.

"Listen," he appealed, edging closer to his father's elbow. "Don't be sore at her if she's nervous when we get there, huh?"

"Sore?" Mark glanced up at him impatiently. "She's got every right in the world to be worried sick if I don't bring you home on time. Do you think I'd do that to her and then get *sore?*" In a minute he tried to sound calmer. "David, go fishing, will you? I don't need you here any more."

David faded back toward the rear of the truck. He knew when he'd been shooed away for being a nuisance. But at least there wasn't going to be any blow-up when they got home. And maybe if Mark had let him discuss it a little more he could have told him a few more things about Mother, and how to understand her. Then if David could just get *her* to listen to what he'd discovered about trying things beyond your strength—

But she'd probably shuck him off, too. More gently, of course. "David, dear, have you done your homework yet?" The whole trouble was—he stared off at the looming tower of darkening cloud—the trouble was they *both* kept thinking he was too young. For everything.

And I'm not. I'm pretty old already. Hastily he dragged out the fishing box and yanked it open. Picked a pink-and-brown fly out of it. *They don't even know how much older I am. And there isn't much time left to prove it!* David jerked the hat down over his eyes and started for the river.

Chapter 17

So you find things out the hard way without anybody teaching you. You find out you can't cast in under the willows where that fish was.

Every time David tried, his hook got caught on the branches and he had to go untangle it. After a few attempts he was sure any fish would have gotten suspicious and gone somewhere else. Maybe to those other willows across the stream. They probably had plenty of pink bugs on them. If he could just get his fly over there a little above them, the current would carry it down under the branches.

He walked back up the bank a way and tried. But to cast clear across he'd have to wade out ten feet or more. He'd known all the time it was going to come to this. Ever since he'd left the truck he had

135

been bracing inside, getting ready for this moment.

Only a little time and everything at stake. *Everything's going to be over if I don't catch a fish.* Mark had said that nobody should deny you the chance to get your own food. And didn't he say, "When you're old enough you'll decide—"? *You're doggone right I'm going to wade out in that water!*

David stood on the bank, deciding just where to step down. Not so easy to see bottom, now. Glossy as a mirror, the river just gave back the overcast of the sky. The thunderhead had moved in across the mountains; it was coming on fast. David could see its insides boiling, as if it were ravenous too.

Mostly he wasn't upset by storms, though he'd never been right out in a bad one. The only thing he wished was that the sun would come back for a minute and show him the bottom of the stream. Then, even as he hesitated, there was a swirl out there in the current—he caught sight of a flash of white. And another, over near the far bank—he glimpsed the whole curve of a rippling shape. Fish rising. Everywhere.

David cast his line as far as he could, but the fly still fell short of the swift water. Holding his breath, he eased down into the shallows. Ice-cold—the shock of it went through the blue jeans. It was a little deeper than he'd thought, halfway to his knees. He took two steps out from the bank and gravel shifted slightly under his sneakers. For a few seconds he stood still, to let his heart catch up—it was all out of time.

Standing down here in the water, he felt like part of the river—it was all around him. From upstream it came pouring down at him, flowing around his legs, bubbling, pulling at them, then sliding away between its banks. He could see rocks downstream bigger than he'd reckoned—huge boulders that split the current. And on beyond, a fast stretch where the water tumbled furiously.

As he stood faltering, with memory tearing and tugging at him, David could almost hear his mother's voice cry out, " . . . too young!" He shrank back. But what would he have to show for it if he gave up? In a few hours Mark would be gone; there'd never be another time to prove anything. *Go on!* he yelled at himself, to drown out the echo of fear.

Strength came differently this time—not as a quick spurt of fire, but more like something cool, thrusting upward through his slenderness. David inched out into the stream. Planted his feet. As he drew back his rod he was concentrating, trying to get the right feel. There was a rhythm, Mark had said. Back

137

easy, line straightens out in the air, flip forward and the rod sends it on curving across the water. It was the best cast he'd made yet.

Still short, though. Feeling his way, step by step, David waded deeper. The current was a moving wall against his legs; he had to lean against it. But this time the fly was out there in the riffle, a pink dot riding the swift water down toward the willows. A fish made a flurry at it, but David didn't feel the strike. Intently he coaxed. With little jerks on the line he jigged the fly as he had seen Mark do. Finally had to draw it in to cast again. Don't put it twice in the same place, Mark had said. Keeping his line whipping in the air David edged downstream a foot, another foot, and set the fly down in a new eddy.

The water was turning dark. He risked a look at the sky—dirty as tarnished metal. A tricky little wind came suddenly down the river, roughing the surface, scattering this way and that. And right behind it came the rain. A long gray fringe trailing from the clouds, it swept the floor of the valley.

But I can't stop now! David glanced around him— fish were going crazy. A little one jumped clear out of the water for no reason at all. There were splashes all over the river.

He cast again—and a white flash sent the air cracking down onto him, breath jammed in his throat.

138

David thought the bolt of lightning must have hit his hook—the rod bucked so hard he had to hang on with both hands as thunder burst against the earth. When it rumbled off, the reel was making a high screech as his line went spinning out. It reached the end, and far downstream a fish shot up out of the water. Arching, flinging itself this way and that. David stared at its antics, and then, as the rod kept plunging in his hands, it dawned on him. The fish was his.

A big one! A really big one. In a frenzy he tried to think what to do. Clamped a finger down on the lever of the automatic reel but nothing happened. The fish was fighting too hard for the reel to begin to bring it in. Tip of the rod was bent to the breaking point—frantically he lowered it some so that it wouldn't snap. But the trout was yanking and ripping around out there, wanting more line. And there wasn't any more to let out. He never knew fish were so strong. Carrying on like that, it was going to bust the thin leader where the fly was tied on. All David could do was go with it, downstream. Had to go fairly fast, slipping on the rocky bottom, just barely keeping his footing.

The willows were right ahead—he didn't know how deep the water was under them, but it had gurgled deep. The whole surface of the stream was pitted with rain now. It was falling hard, stinging cold. Worst of all, it chewed up the water so that you couldn't see an inch into it.

Then when he was nearly up to his waist, the fish let up its wild thrashing and lay still. Heavy as a chunk of iron out there on the end of his line, but it seemed to be tiring. With his left hand David tried to pull it in—slowly it came. Grudgingly, kicking a little, the fish let itself be hauled closer and closer, as David carefully fed the line back onto his reel a few inches at a time. Whenever the trout struggled, David waited. It was only thirty feet from him, then twenty. In the seething water where it floundered he caught a glimpse of a blunt head with an underslung jaw. And big—!

As he reached out to draw it toward him once more, all fury broke loose. The trout hurtled high out of the water, skittering on its tail an instant, then plunged and darted for the opposite bank. All the line went screaming off his reel again, burning his hand. When the fish hit the end, it charged upstream, broke out of the water once more, then came back down so fast he didn't know where it was until the rod was almost ripped from his grip. The fish was there below the willows again—pulling hard.

He took another step downstream, the current tugging him along. Abruptly the gravel was slipping, slip-

140

ping, washing from under his feet. A cold torrent swept over his head—David was flung along, tumbled, swirled. Blindly he fought out, struggling—free of the current and got his head up, gasping for breath. Floundering over to a rock, he clung there. The rod was still clenched in his hand, but when he tried his line it was slack.

Numbly he blinked the water off his lashes. Couldn't get located. There was the clump of willows—above him. He must have been carried right under the branches. He slumped against the boulder, breathing hard, the rain pelting down on him. Lightning still splintered across the sky, but the thunder already sounded gone—on off across the wild high country.

After a while David waded the rest of the way to the bank. He felt as heavy as wet wash. With chilled fingers he hooked the pink fly to the handle of the rod. Had to find Mark's hat . . . he spotted it a little way below, floating in a backwash.

The flies were still stuck in the band, but the hat itself was sodden. He shook some of the water from it. For a minute he stood there, trying to put some shape back into it, but it was no use. He was just sorry it had got so wet. Terribly sorry.

Grieving silently, David started back, carrying the hat and rod. He wished he didn't have to tell Mark

all about it, but he supposed he would. No amount of rain could make him this soggy. It was letting up now, dwindled to a sprinkle. He started to cut across the field toward the truck, when something got through the haze of his defeat. The pickup was turned facing homeward. But the front seat was empty. He glanced around.

Over by the river, on that same big rock, Mark sat—watching him. As David walked over, shoes squelching at every step, he knew he wasn't going to have to tell his father much. Mark had seen the whole thing.

Chapter 18

No telling what Mark was thinking. One ragged brow cocked higher than the other, as he might look at something he'd never seen before. Must have been sitting here right through the storm to get that drenched. Water stood out in drops on the bristling pale hair. His shirt was plastered to his muscular shoulders—he'd taken off the windbreaker and wrapped it around his injured foot. Now he sat, waiting.

Well, there was only one way to do this. David walked straight up, close enough to be reached. He met the steady look of those burnt blue eyes as he said, "I waded out in the water. I had to."

Mark nodded.

"I didn't know when you'd get the truck fixed—"

"It was the fuses," Mark said. "They'd blown out. Never thought of it until you were talking just now. After I changed those, everything worked."

"Well, I didn't know. And we needed food—"

"You don't have to explain to me."

"Well, you told me not to do it. And I'm sorry. But—"

"—you had to. Under certain rare circumstances that's enough reason."

David fell silent. Mark didn't seem angry. Just kept looking at him strangely.

"I fell in!" David insisted. "I got all wet. And I lost a fish."

"I know." Mark glanced downstream and for an instant fear shadowed his face, as if he were seeing it all over again. But when he looked back at David there was a spark of pride in his eyes. "That was a good one you had on."

Which just made it worse. Mark thought it was a good, big fish, too. "It doesn't do any good if you lose it." David remembered the hat and held it out. "I guess that's ruined."

Mark took it from him. "It's been this wet before." He was scanning the flies in the band. "Which one were you using?"

"A pink one. I got it out of your box." He held out his rod and showed it to Mark. "I had a silly idea, because I found this bug—" David dug it out of his pocket, fairly squashed.

Mark held it in his palm as if it were valuable. "I'll be darned. I never saw a salmon fly up here this early in the year."

"It was on those willows. I heard a fish snap at it, but I couldn't cast under there. I don't know how. I just messed it up every time."

"That's a tough one." Mark reached down and picked up his own rod which had been lying in the grass beside the rock. Shaking loose the line, he began to let it out, flicking the rod back and forth until he had a good length stroking through the air over his head. "First get your distance"— he sent the line reaching out toward a bush that overhung the stream below. His hook almost touched it and came whipping back—"then let it drop." He set the fly down lightly in the water as if it had just fluttered off the bush. "That takes practice—plenty of practice. Better at first to work the fast water, just as you did."

"I wasn't working anything." The big hope was finished anyhow. No point trying to act as if he was a hero now. "I was standing there all out of breath from that lightning and the fish got on my line. I didn't even know it was there at first."

Mark just looked more interested. "If that's how it happened, you did some quick thinking to handle

147

him as well as you did. Where did you get the idea to go downstream with him?"

"Well, he was going to break the line if I didn't!"

"Right. But most people haul back on their first fish and try to drag him in by main strength. You played him." Mark's voice was rising hotly.

"He was the one playing!" David hollered. "He ran all around me. I didn't even know where he was."

"For not knowing you sure kept a tight line. What are you trying to do, sell me the idea you can't fish?" Mark pointed a finger at him. "You're going to be a crackerjack fisherman. Don't kid me!"

They eyed each other an instant. Mark's mouth quirked, then broke into a grin—the one-sided hungry grin that had haunted David's dreams. But he couldn't remember why he had wanted to run from it. Now he just wished he could wrestle Mark good, thump him and grin back. But shyness still gripped him. Even if Mark did think he had done all right—

"I wouldn't mind it getting away so much if we didn't need it," he said stiffly.

"I know. When you feel as if you're on trial"— Mark was serious again— "you want to be at your best. And your best can get all crossed up like a bunch of hot wires. One chance, and only a little time to use it—you think if you're worth anything you should be able to pull a miracle out of a hat when you need one." He shook his head. "Doesn't work that way, does it?"

It was so much what David had been thinking, it took him a minute to realize that Mark was talking about himself.

"Did you lose a fish too?" he wondered.

It took his father a minute to hear the question. "A fish? No—that's one of the few things I seem to know something about." Reaching down, he picked up the end of a string. Out of the shallows he pulled a cluster of medium-sized trout, all cleaned, ready for the pan. As David gaped at them, he smiled wryly.

"You aren't hungry, are you? Come on, let's go build a fire."

It was like reaching into a mirror, trading places with another self. David could hardly believe that Mark had said those words in just that way, exactly as he had planned it himself. Had Mark felt the same wish, too—that they could patch up the pieces of this weekend somehow? That he just *had* to do something before it was too late? It must have been that, to make him come clear over to the river on that injured leg. Mark had needed those fish he'd caught! Even worse than David had wanted that one of his! It made David feel years older as he thought about it—and what it meant.

It meant that the last hope wasn't quite finished between them! Not if he could just say the right thing. Because here they were, making their way slowly toward the truck, Mark's arm clamped hard around his shoulders—they'd never been this close before. The sun was beginning to break through the shredding clouds. In a minute they would be sitting down across a fire from each other, eating those trout. It was the chance he had pictured all along. If nothing else went wrong now—

But Mark had a funny look on his face. As they reached the truck he was beginning to feel in his pockets. From his shirt he took a damp pack of cigarettes and some wet matches. Tossing them aside, he began to search through the junk on the floor of the pickup. The tailgate he had left down; right inside were the tackle box and some scattered tools.

"There wasn't any point closing it with the food gone!" Mark was staring in open dismay. "Who'd ever think—?"

It was bad, whatever it was. David couldn't see anything to make Mark groan like that.

"What's wrong?"

"I left it right here!" Mark turned over the tools, shoving things around some more. "I put the smokes in my pocket and took out those few matches—"

It must be the matchbox he was hunting for. It was a metal cylinder—one of the waterproof kind. David started to scrummage for it, too. If they had lost that . . . !

"Never mind." Mark sounded beat. "It's gone. And I know who took it." He picked something up—handed it to David. A small round stone.

Chapter 19

The fire hissed and crackled. It was smoking just enough to smell good. The frying pan hadn't been washed after breakfast yesterday morning, so the aroma of bacon rose around the sizzling fish. And Mark kept looking at David as if he had produced those matches by black magic.

It had been about the best minute in David's life. While Mark stood there sunk, just to haul out the old jacket and reach in the pocket: "Here, I've got some." Like it was nothing at all.

Now as he leaned forward to turn the fish David was remembering those frightened minutes when he had hidden the matches away for some dark emergency. He hoped his father would never find out how terrified he had been.

152

But Mark was suspicious. "Do you always carry matches?"

"No, sir. Just on fishing trips."

"David, you're hiding something from me."

"Well—I was going to tell you—" David seized a chance to change the subject. "That's exactly the same way I lost your spinners. I left them there on the tailgate for a few minutes and when I got back, there were two stones." It still seemed crazy that the mystery which had made him so uneasy should turn out to be the work of a nosy little creature a few inches long. It made him feel foolish. "Do you reckon the packrat could have taken my can of ham, too?"

Mark nodded. "If there was a stone left in its place, he's the culprit. A camp robber or a magpie will steal your bright stuff, too. But nothing except a packrat leaves a pebble behind."

David grinned. It had just occurred to him, to picture that darn-fool animal sitting down in its hole surrounded by two spinners, a can of ham, and a box of matches. "You reckon the stones were his way of paying for things?"

"Who knows? Maybe he thought you wouldn't miss what he took. I've never figured it out, but those little thieves have robbed me before. I should have known better than to leave that matchbox out."

Mark was beginning to look disgusted with himself again.

Hurriedly David said, "If it wasn't for your fish, we wouldn't have needed any matches."

His father smiled a little. "You'll get that big bruiser of yours, someday. You'll come back up here and go to the same spot and stalk him. I've done it myself, even years later. You never quite get over a big fish that fights free."

"What do you do if he keeps taking you down the river and there's a deep hole like that? You can't go on and you can't pull him in?"

"If it was me I'd get below the willows before I cast, then put the fly upstream as far as possible. Keep planning where you'll land a fish even before you hook one. I could show you—" There was that quickening sound in his voice, then it went flat again.

"Well, you'll find it all out by experience. I did."

"It's kind of lonesome, though, to be up here *all* by yourself."

"I think those fish are done," Mark said.

They ate right out of the frying pan. Sitting knee to knee, they dug into the meal silently. David couldn't even think beyond the taste of those first few bites.

" . . . good . . . " he breathed as he ate. Then glancing up at Mark, he said it again, acutely. "This is *good!*"

Mark was watching him, not eating much himself. "At least it makes up a little for this rough time we've had."

David scooped up another forkful. "It's been a good time, all of it."

"Your mother wouldn't think so."

David gulped. Twice. Because here it was, the thing they had to talk about. And he hadn't figured it yet. "Well, she'll be a little scared about the bears," he began earnestly, "but—"

"No need for her to know about that. When we get home, I'll drop you off. You won't have to go into the whole story; it would just frighten her."

"If she understands everything it won't."

"You may want to come up here again someday, when you're older. Better skip the gory details."

"She'll let us come up," David insisted, "because I'm older now. I'm going to tell her about that."

Mark shook his head. "You are, but that doesn't cut much ice with a grizzly. That's what she'll be afraid of."

"We'll *explain*. We'll tell her it's kind of dangerous, but anyhow we have to come back. You know, we just have to."

Mark stared down at the frayed bandages on his foot. "I know, and it's true. You will have to when the time comes. Right now I can sympathize with her more than I ever did before. Watching you fall in that river took ten years off my life."

It surprised David. He had almost forgotten his own fear of the water. Somehow it had washed away when he'd gone under.

"Well, I came up again all right."

His father nodded. "But did you know that if that bolt of lightning had struck the stream it could electrocute you on the spot?"

David considered that.

"Suppose the water had swept you onto the rocks and you'd hit your head? I saw my own kid brother go down—" Mark looked away into some far-off past.

David held still inside. For memory was coming to the surface fast now. He could hear his father's voice, years back in time, saying angrily, "My brother drowned because he couldn't swim. This boy's going to learn!" And the strong hands had seized him, swung him out over some dark water. His mother had screamed. It had been the worst of all those early times. And yet as he sat here, so near his father, none of the fear came back.

"We'd better tell her." David hardly knew he said it aloud.

"What?"

"Something else we have to tell Mother. That this is the first time I ever used my swimming, and it's different from the YMCA pool."

"You're doggone right it is!"

"But it's still O.K. That's what we have to tell her."

Mark sat back wearily, rubbing his eyes. "Your mother and I had quite a—difference over that question once. I wanted you to learn how to react to a plunge into cold water. When you were just a baby I wanted to try it, while I was around to pull you out if you needed help. So you might be able later on to handle yourself when I wasn't there. She said it would frighten you too much. She was probably right—I don't know. It's been years . . . "

"Yeah," David said quickly, "that was a long time ago. Let's go home, Mark."

It took quite a while to drive out of the forest.

Mark's knuckles stood out bony, he was holding the wheel so tightly. He could work the clutch with his hurt foot, but he had to take it easy. Which was all right—it gave David time to figure what he was going to say to his mother. You can't just bust right out and tell her: "Mark needs to come back to us. He's lonesome."

When they got to the highway he still didn't have it figured. "How long do you reckon it'll take us to get to the city?" he asked absently.

"Three or four hours at this rate," Mark said. "Look in the glove compartment, will you? My watch is there."

It was full of stuff. When David rummaged in it, a wallet fell out. As he picked it up, it opened in his hand and there was his mother. She looked like a young girl, with her hair all loose around her cheeks and her eyes shining. She was smiling, a beautiful look, at whoever snapped the picture. Mark glanced over—when he saw it he seemed disconcerted. Took the wallet and shoved it in his pocket as if it were pretty private.

David found the watch. "It's five-thirty."

"We're not going to make it by seven. I guess I'd better call her." In front of the gas station ahead there was a public phone booth. Mark pulled over to it.

158

"Let me talk to her," David asked urgently. That picture had told him how to go ahead. If she was *in love* with Mark, the rest ought to be easy.

His father thought it over. "Maybe that would be a good idea. If she hears your voice she'll be sure you're all right." He gave David some change. It didn't take long. In just a minute she was there— the "hello" sounded worried.

"Hi," David called to her briskly.

"Oh, Davey! Where are you?" Pleased, but anxious.

"We're still up on the pass. Listen, Mother, it was great! We got chased by a bear and I fell in the river." You get that kind of news over with first. "It was a grizzly bear, too. She ate all our food. Mother?"

"Yes," she said faintly. "Yes, I'm listening."

"Well, Mark got kind of hurt. The bear clawed him. Have you got some bandages and things?"

By that time Mark had got himself out of the truck and hobbled to the booth. "What are you—? David, give me the phone!"

"He's bleeding pretty bad," David finished. "Here he is—"

He got back in the pickup. That ought to do it. She always got soft all over when people were bleeding. He could hear Mark stammering around.

"No, no, it looks worse than it is. No, Jeanne,

159

I'm all right. Well, we did run into some trouble, but you've got a boy who can take it. He's a credit to you—" Then he saw David listening and shut the door of the phone booth.

They talked for a long time—Mark had to get out some more change. David let his head tip back against the seat. He was thinking of the grizzly, way off somewhere quiet.

When Mark finally came back he looked warm. But not too unhappy, though he was trying to act severe. "Now she'll sit there imagining the worst, for hours. You shouldn't have gone into all that over the phone."

"What did you tell her?" David asked curiously.

"I tried to calm her down. It wasn't easy. I may have to go in with you after all, just to prove that I'm not dying."

"Yeah." David smiled innocently.

As they drove on down he was thinking. Next time, they'd bring Mother with them up to the mountains; they'd find a place she'd enjoy so that she wouldn't be afraid any more. But the valley, with the stream running through—all by itself now except for the big fish cruising in it—he hoped that would keep on being something just between him and Mark.

HARPER TROPHY BOOKS
you will enjoy reading

HARPER & ROW, PUBLISHERS, INC.
10 East 53rd Street, New York, New York 10022

DATE DUE